"I'm all wrong for you, Joe. What's between us is just chemistry," Ellen protested.

"Chemistry is for labs, Ell. I'm in love with you."

"No!" She froze, his words swirling in her brain.

"That's what you're really afraid of, isn't it? That's what's making you push me away. Love. You love me."

It couldn't be true. After all that had happened, she should be immune to love. "I . . . I can't."

"You can't. Not you *don't*." His eyes were blazing. "Not you don't. Say it."

She clamped her lips shut against a further giveaway. She couldn't say it, couldn't tell him the truth.

"Say it," he demanded.

"I love you," she shouted. "Now let me go!"

"Never." His mouth found hers in a scorching kiss. . . .

WHAT ARE *LOVESWEPT* ROMANCES?

They are stories of true romance and touching emotion. We believe those two very important ingredients are constants in our highly sensual and very believable stories in the *LOVESWEPT* line. Our goal is to give you, the reader, stories of consistently high quality that may sometimes make you laugh, sometimes make you cry, but are always fresh and creative and contain many delightful surprises within their pages.

Most romance fans read an enormous number of books. Those they truly love, they keep. Others may be traded with friends and soon forgotten. We hope that each *LOVESWEPT* romance will be a treasure—a "keeper." We will always try to publish

LOVE STORIES YOU'LL NEVER FORGET
BY AUTHORS YOU'LL ALWAYS REMEMBER

The Editors

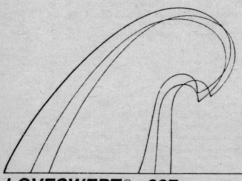

LOVESWEPT® · 337

Linda Cajio
Desperate Measures

 BANTAM BOOKS
NEW YORK · TORONTO · LONDON · SYDNEY · AUCKLAND

DESPERATE MEASURES

A Bantam Book / July 1989

*If you would be interested in receiving protective vinyl
covers for your Loveswept books, please write to this address
for information:*

*Loveswept
Bantam Books
P.O. Box 985
Hicksville, NY 11802*

ISBN 0-553-22011-X

*Bill Flannery—who
made his own
"emergency" exit.
Thanks for the
inspiration.*

One

___

She was the most incredible woman he'd ever seen.

At least he thought she was, Joe Carlini admitted as he desperately tried to keep his balance and look natural. Still, his frantic glance around the roller skating rink had shown someone extraordinary.

"Dammit. Of all times," he said under his breath, while gingerly placing one skate in front of the other. Naturally, there would be a major distraction when he was trying to prevent a catastrophe. His feet slipped out in opposite directions yet again, and he clutched at the lime green cinder-block wall. Muttering curses, he managed to stay upright through sheer willpower.

He decided he was insane to have thought he could pull this off. The last time he'd been on skates was at least twenty years ago, and he hadn't been any good at it then. He certainly wasn't fooling any of the adults at this southern New Jersey skating rink. All of them were whizzing gracefully by him with the skills of experience and practice . . . including Mario Penza.

This was no time to be clinging to cinder block, Joe thought, as he inched his way along the wall. He had followed his adversary to the rink without a hitch, then had boldly come inside. Mario, to his reluctant admiration, had barely blinked at the opposition's unexpected appearance. It had been a fluke of luck that Joe had discovered Mario's rendezvous . . . and he'd been horrified when he realized what Mario was up to. Still, Joe had won this particular battle, and Mario's clever attempt at espionage was in jeopardy. Up to a point. Unfortunately, it was an "adults only" morning at the rink, with free coffee and doughnuts, so a nonskater drew more attention to himself than he might want. But why Joe had thought *he* would be less conspicuous on skates was beyond him now. He had hoped, in one stroke, to trap Mario and whomever he was meeting. Instead, he had fallen into another trap quite nicely.

Mario's voice was suddenly in his ear. "You're not as smart as everyone thinks you are, Joe."

Ignoring the sarcasm, Joe turned his head toward Mario, who had braked to a halt a mere foot away. Joe smiled blandly. He knew he couldn't show the least emotion. "So you would like to think."

Mario was not daunted. "You look so foolish."

"Not as foolish as you are. You've been caught, Mario."

The young face lost its cocky expression and turned hard. "You can't do a damn thing without proof and you know it. And if you do, I'll rub your nose in it."

"And you've just admitted there's proof to be had," Joe said.

Mario snarled at his own mistake, then skated away. Joe grimaced as he watched him go. Knowing Mario—and unfortunately he knew him all too well—Joe was certain the younger man would hardly be chastened by the exchange. Joe muttered a barnyard curse that summed up all his frustrations beautifully.

"Instead of swearing at the fates, why don't you keep me company while I skate over to the benches?"

The voice was soft and serene and tinged with amusement. Even before he turned his head, Joe knew whom he would find.

Still, he wasn't prepared for his own reaction when he stared into her blue-green eyes. The internal explosion was instantaneous and intense, and like nothing he'd ever felt before.

His first thought was that his first thought hadn't done her justice. She was very beautiful. And then he realized she wasn't. At least not in the conventional sense. Her jaw was a shade too square and her nose a shade too broad for her features to be truly delicate. But her complexion was flawless, the fair skin like rich, unblemished cream. Her hair, pulled back from her face, was neither brown nor blond. More of a champagne color, he decided. Her perfume was subtle and clearly expensive. His gaze wandered helplessly downward to discover breasts, soft and full, a small waist, and rounded hips. The gentle slenderness of her body was undeniably sensual.

And best of all, she had a thoroughly kissable mouth.

Some shred of sense surfaced, reminding him he was there to prevent the course of destruction set by Mario. But his awareness was caught by the answering fire flaring in her eyes. He blindly reached out his hand to it. . . .

And, incredibly, it was gone.

"Can you go with me?" she asked in the most normal of voices. "Or would you prefer to hang onto the wall?"

Her sensual response to him had been so brief, he almost wondered if he had imagined it. He couldn't have. Still, she had suppressed it so completely. . . .

Joe cleared his throat and straightened. His skates instantly shot out from under him. The woman grabbed his arm and steadied him before he lost his balance. He was surprised and yet not surprised that her touch ignited a slow burn within him. It radiated through his veins, heating his blood.

Whoever she was, she did the damnedest things to him. And he very much liked the way she avoided embarrassing him. She looked familiar too. He wondered if he'd seen her before, yet knew he wouldn't have forgotten if he had.

"I think I'll try the benches," he said, grinning. "I thought this would be like riding a bicycle and everything would instantly come back."

"I believe that is the theory," she replied, smiling at him.

"I'm Joe Carlini."

Her smile faded for an instant. "I . . . my name is Ellen, and I find waddling like a duck helps."

Joe blinked, not sure he heard right. "You waddle like a duck?"

"Yes. Here, I'll show you." Her fingers tightened around his arm. She bent her knees slightly and pushed off slowly from side to side. He helplessly followed her example. He had to, or else he'd be pulling her down with him. While the thought had its merits, he didn't care to make a fool of himself voluntarily. He was doing just fine involuntarily.

He realized that his feet *weren't* slipping out from under him and his balance was much better.

"I can skate!" he exclaimed.

"Maybe it would be best not to commit yourself quite so soon," Ellen cautioned, when he wavered.

"Good point."

Still, he couldn't help gazing around the skating rink with newfound pleasure. He spotted Mario and immediately reminded himself he was here to stop the younger man from conducting his "business." He had to. The consequences were unthinkable if he didn't.

Mario was staring back. Joe couldn't quite make out his expression from across the wooden rink, but the other was so intent on him that he nearly bumped into a skating couple. After neatly avoiding the collision, Mario dipped his head in concession. Joe nodded back, indicating their "game" was hardly over. He hated to impose upon his lovely rescuer further, but he had no choice. It was an opportunity he couldn't afford to waste.

With more courage than he thought he had he

steered away from the benches and toward the skating circle.

"You're going in the wrong direction," Ellen warned.

"More fool I," he said, taking her hand. He skated just a little faster, and when he didn't fall on his face, he said, "Actually, I'm getting a lot of self-confidence back, so if you'd just hang in here with me for a few turns around the rink, I'd really appreciate it. I feel like I'm on a roll."

"Let's not get crazy here." She hesitated for a moment, then laughed slightly. "More fool I. But only once around the rink, and then we'll see."

He heard an underlying surprise in her laugh, as if she hadn't laughed for a long time. He glanced at her. Now that the fire he'd glimpsed earlier was under control, he could discern an air of fragility about her, as though she were close to shattering. The thought startled him. He tightened his fingers around hers and smiled. "Good. I'll lead."

He sped up his "waddle." He wouldn't win any races, he admitted, but at least he was moving at more than a snail's pace . . . and staying upright. This wasn't so bad.

"Been skating long?" he asked his companion, as he noticed Mario weaving expertly in and out of the other skaters. Show-off, he thought darkly.

Ellen didn't answer at first. He glanced over at her patrician profile. She must have sensed his awareness, for she said, "I skate off and on. It's great exercise."

"So I've been told. Unfortunately, somebody forgot to tell me about the pitfalls."

She groaned at his near pun. "You're doing very well."

"I'm getting great help," he said, squeezing her fingers. Her hand fitted in his perfectly, as if made for it. "I thought I'd try this rather than the gym," he added. "It seemed . . . easier. I forgot that you actually had to know how to skate."

She laughed, and again he sensed a rustiness on her part. He was also beginning to sense a barrier, very subtle yet solid. She was politely friendly and no more.

And that, he thought, as Mario skated across their path, was all he had time for right now.

"Do you come here often?" he asked, hoping she might have seen Mario here before. At the moment he was desperate for any kind of information.

"Oh . . . ahh," she stammered. He was surprised to see color flushing her cheeks. "I've been here once or twice, maybe. Actually, hardly ever."

Somehow her words didn't ring true. It was obvious she skated regularly somewhere, although he knew it might not be at this rink. He decided another tack might be better.

"I wouldn't think so many people could get away on a weekday morning to skate," he said, and pointed to Mario. "Take that guy. Somehow he doesn't look like a guy who would skate."

Ellen smiled. "Neither do you."

"You're telling me," he mumbled. He watched Mario skate up to a man, pause there for a second, then move past. He'd done this several times with various people. Joe's heart lifted with hope each time, only to be dashed when no flick of anything passed between them. Dammit, which one was *the* one? With a vague suspicion that he was being taunted, he resumed his probing of Ellen. "But he can really skate, can't he? Ever seen him here before, Ellen?"

Somebody accidentally bumped into Ellen before she could answer, and she was pushed just far enough away for their hands to break contact. Instantly he felt as insecure as ever on the skates, and he stretched out his hand to take hers again.

He missed.

Joe yelped as he felt his body overbalance. He forced himself up, and overbalanced in the opposite direction. He tried to keep his backside as far from the hard wooden floor as possible. His feet shot forward of their own accord.

"Waddle!" Ellen shouted from behind him.

He waddled. He was able to bring his balance back, but the waddling had an unfortunate side effect. His speed had increased, and he was zooming between the skaters and the outer wall of the rink at a pace Jackie Stewart would have admired. He passed his cousin at a fast clip. He had no idea how to stop, and there was nothing to grab onto to brake himself.

He was considering crashing into the wall when he caught sight of a bar sticking out from it at about waist height. His mind registered that it was one of the emergency exit doors. Blessing the miracle, he grabbed for it as he approached. His fingers closed gratefully around the cold steel.

To his horror, the bar gave inward.

The exit door swung open, and Joe shot out into the blinding spring sunlight. He rolled across the concrete sidewalk . . . and fell flat on his face the moment his roller skates hit the grass. He lay there, face down in the dandelions, and decided he was really going to have to talk to Mario about his choice of illicit rendezvous. A nice, safe hotel lounge would have done very well. He could hear voices behind him, and he reluctantly sat up. Nothing seemed to be broken except his dignity. A group of skaters were crowded in the open doorway.

"Leaving so soon?" someone asked.

"I have a plane to catch," Joe quipped, and everyone laughed.

"You should turn in your skates first, mister," the rink manager said with amusement.

"I told the skates that, but they wouldn't listen," Joe said, chuckling.

Several people helped him to his feet and back into the building. Once he was settled onto one of the benches, out of harm's way, everyone skated off. He looked around, puzzled for a moment and not sure why.

"What's wrong with this picture?" he muttered.

Then he realized that Mario, formerly so visible among the other skaters, had vanished. He was nowhere to be seen inside the skating rink.

And neither was the beautiful Ellen.

"You *will* be coming to the charity dance for Graduate Hospital, won't you, Ellen?"

Ellen Kitteridge turned her mind from the unwanted image of a sexy man with a devastating smile. That image had haunted her for three days.

Her almost uncontrollable reaction to Joe Carlini had been vivid. And frightening.

Spotting her grandmother's willful expression, she hid a smile. Trust Lettice Kitteridge to turn a question into a command.

"We'll see, Grandmother," she said, and sipped her after-lunch coffee. The dance was a good cause, but she hated the thought of all those people knowing . . . and staring . . .

"I'm on the board of trustees," her grandmother said, exasperation evident in her voice. "People expect it of you."

"That's nice."

"You came to Marlee's tea the other day."

"Yes, I did," Ellen said, then tapped the seven heavily embossed envelopes next to her napkin. "Marlee asked me as a friend, not because my name looks good on the guest list. Which is more than I can say for these. And you know as well as I do the phone-call invitations are double this every day. Everybody wants the former wife of Prince Florian Borghese at their party or tea. But nobody will actually talk to Ellen Kitteridge, who had the nerve to divorce 'Italy's Darling.' "

The delicate cup in her grandmother's hand met the saucer with a sharp click. She raised her chin to a disapproving angle. "Really, Ellen, you do yourself a disservice. Everybody—"

"Everybody, including my parents, has made it a point to show their disappointment that I had a shot at being this generation's Grace Kelly and I blew it."

"I told you not to marry him," Lettice said.

Ellen stifled a moan. Hoping to head off the

lecture, she said in a rush, "Yes, and you were the only one. And I was a fool not to listen to you. Could we end this now?"

"Yes, you were a fool," Lettice agreed, clearly ignoring her granddaughter's request. "He was an overblown ski bum with some dingy title, and you fell for it."

"He was hardly a ski bum. He'd won gold medals in the giant slalom in two consecutive Olympics. And his family have been princes of Lombardy since the middle ages." Ellen knew she was fueling her grandmother, yet she felt, in all fairness, she had to mention the truth.

Lettice made a rude noise. "Big deal. You were too shy to stand up for yourself in those days, and too eager to please. With my idiot son pushing you like that, it was no wonder you fell for that hulking blond. Everybody was enamored of that title, but nobody considered that the man didn't measure up to it. You did measure up as a princess, however. I was very proud of the way you took on all those duties he couldn't be bothered with. I know you didn't care for the socializing that your position required. You were admirable, child."

"Thank you." Ellen toyed with her napkin. It was amazing how many hospital dedications and school openings could be attended in one day. But all of it had fit in with what everyone expected of her, and she'd thought she'd finally found her niche as Florian's wife.

Unfortunately, she had been naive enough to believe a sensitive, loving man had been hiding behind his "playboy prince" image. But then she'd discovered that the Borghese estate needed financial shoring up. Worse, Florian ran through money like water and actually thrived on gossip and publicity. She had later thought that he must have picked women who were on a tabloid's payroll— the stories of his affairs had been detailed, sensational, and published almost daily. Florian had actually kept a scrapbook. It had taken a tragedy for her to swallow her pride at last and admit that Florian had definitely gone for the gold. Hers.

"At least you wised up, packed up your bank accounts, and came home," her grandmother said.

Ellen closed her eyes as the familiar, sharp pain of loss ripped through her. The price for that wisdom had been terrible. She would gladly have continued to sacrifice her pride and dignity to Florian if she hadn't lost her son, Paulo. But whatever dreams or hopes she'd had crumbled, and she had come home divorced and disgraced. Only the very conventional Lettice Kitteridge had surprised everyone and stood by her granddaughter's side. Since then, Ellen had been content to drift.

"There you go blanking out again!" Lettice snapped.

Ellen opened her eyes to find her grandmother glaring at her.

Lettice went on. "I know everyone acted like an idiot about the accident and your divorce. Especially that boneheaded son of mine. Good thing he and your mother have taken to living in Palm Beach year round now. My blood still boils when I think of the way they've both cut you off." Lettice clamped her jaw shut.

"I'm sorry I caused a rift between you and my father," Ellen said in a low voice.

Lettice rapped a spoon against the table. "Don't be silly, Ellen. I've told you before: When they handed out brains, your father was in the short line. Your mother too. None of us have gotten along for years. When I think of the genes you could have inherited . . . Now that was a real crapshoot. Fortunately, you came up a winner."

Chuckling, Ellen shook her head.

"Still, back to my point," Lettice said. "You've had a right to hide yourself away after all that's happened. But you've been moping around ever since you came back from Europe. It's about time you stopped being depressed, Ellen, and pulled yourself up by the bootstraps."

Ellen started laughing. She couldn't help it. Her grandmother's eyebrows rose in surprise.

"Only you would order someone out of a depression, Grandmother."

"Of course. So you *will* go to the charity dance," Lettice said, bringing Ellen abruptly back to the issue under discussion.

She smiled. It was obvious her grandmother was ready to do battle. She hated to disappoint her, but a charity dance wasn't worth the fight.

"If it will make you happy, then I'll go to the dance."

"Good," her grandmother pronounced with clear satisfaction. "Now, I have an escort in mind—"

"I don't need a date," Ellen said firmly. Her grandmother had tried to fix her up before, but Ellen had no interest in "dates." A little voice inside her suggested one particular man might be a very interesting date. She ignored it. Joe Carlini had literally sailed out the door, and she ought to be grateful for that. One Italian in her life had been more than enough.

"But—"

"Don't push your luck," Ellen said, rising from the luncheon table. She walked around it and kissed the older woman's cheek. "I'll find my own date if I need one, thank you very much."

"I just want you to be happy," Lettice said in an innocent tone.

Ellen shook her head. "Anybody ever tell you you're a manipulator of the first water?"

"I take pride in it, my dear," Lettice said, smiling at her. "You're getting very uppity, you know."

"This family could use another Anne," Ellen said pointedly.

"Heaven forbid!" her grandmother exclaimed. "Your cousin is a trial."

Ellen chuckled. The clashes between her independent cousin and the "matriarch" of the family were notorious. Still, she wished she had some of Anne's courage for confrontation. Instead, she always took the easy route. Like now.

"I suppose it's enough that you've agreed to attend," her grandmother finally said in clear defeat. Obviously, one Anne was enough.

"It's all you're going to get," Ellen said, smiling to take any sting out of her words.

"I'll take it. But you ought to get out more. About the only place you'll go to willingly is that spa of yours."

"Yes, grandmother," Ellen said, her tone meek to cover renewed amusement. It wasn't her fault if

Grandmother assumed her morning excursions were to an Elizabeth Arden's.

The doorbell rang, and Ellen glanced up in surprise. She knew nobody was expected. Shrugging, she said, "I'll get it."

"Mamie will do it," Lettice said.

"Mamie's in the kitchen cleaning up the luncheon dishes," Ellen reminded her. "Sometimes I think you're back in the thirties, Grandmother. I'm surprised you never took President Roosevelt to task for his methods of fixing the Great Depression."

"I did, dear," Lettice said smugly.

"I'll still answer the door."

As she walked to the door, Ellen couldn't keep her thoughts from turning back yet again to the other day. She had been indulging herself at the rink in New Jersey, far from her grandmother's Gladwyne, Pennsylvania, home. That wonderful urge to get on skates and "bop" to the music was one she had acquired in boarding school. It had gotten her into trouble before. Maybe she ought to blame the school for giving her a flamboyant roommate, she thought. Cecilia St. Martin had taught her to skate in the first place.

Now she was older and wiser about the "acceptable." Truthfully, it was nobody's business what she did, but she had no wish to upset her grandmother needlessly. Lettice had firm notions about what was acceptable. Still, rebellion was one thing, privacy quite another.

Ellen swallowed, her steps slowing. But then she had met a man. One very sexy man. At thirty, she had sternly told herself, she should be long past schoolgirl reactions to handsome men. Still, she had rushed out of that rink at the first opportunity, as if the hounds of hell were after her. If ever there was a time to let sleeping dogs lie, this was it. And the dogs had better be deep in dreamland. She had no desire to complicate her life any more than it already was.

At least she'd hung around long enough to see that Joe Carlini had been unhurt, she thought, chuckling as she remembered his grand exit. She knew she shouldn't be laughing, but she couldn't help it. It seemed so long since a man had made her laugh.

A picture of his strong, darkly tanned Roman features flashed across her mind, and she immediately sobered. He *was* good-looking, she admitted. Even without the skates, he would be quite tall. His hair was almost black, which wasn't surprising given his heritage, yet his eyes were an unexpected light brown, nearly hazel. Under his easy exterior, she had sensed a power that came from a man used to being in command.

Ellen groaned as she tried to force her thoughts in another, safer direction before she answered the door. And she tried with even less success to ignore the little voice that said she had had more than help on her mind when she'd first approached Joe at the rink. She wouldn't have left anyone struggling along as he had been. She knew she wouldn't. She'd had to offer help. And then, when she had looked into his eyes, she had been momentarily willing to do anything for him. She understood the expression "like lightning" all too well now. She had been struck.

And she didn't need that, she told herself. Not now, not ever. Hadn't she had a whopper of a lesson about men? She'd even sworn off Italian food, for goodness' sakes! And she certainly wasn't interested in any Americanized version of her ex-husband. Or in any man. She'd had about all the infamy and excitement any person was entitled to.

All she wanted now was peace and quiet. A lot of peace and quiet. She had a feeling that there wouldn't be any with a man like Joe Carlini.

She opened the double front doors to find her wish completely shattered.

Joe Carlini smiled at her.

Two

"Hello, Ellen," he said.

She just stared at him as a jumble of sensations ran through her.

"Aren't you going to say 'Hello, Joe'?" he asked.

"Hello, Joe," she parroted, still in shock. His gray suit and dark blue tie made him more attractive. Too damn attractive. She blinked and tried to pull herself together. And immediately lost it. "How did you find me? I never said . . . Who told you? Nobody could. Nobody knows who I am. I mean nobody at the rink knows who I am."

"They do if they read the papers," he replied. "You shouldn't go to events that make the society column."

"Who thought anyone even glanced at that thing?" she muttered, realizing she had given herself away. It must have been the Children's Burn Center fund-raiser. That was the only public function she'd gone to recently.

"Pardon me?"

"Just cursing the fates."

Joe grinned, and she remembered that she'd said something similar at the rink.

"You were part of the background of the picture they printed," he said. "A very pretty part of it."

"Thank you." The photographer must have had the largest wide angle-lens in existence, she thought. She had been sitting as far away from any picture-taking as possible.

Instantly she pushed the thought away. She should be more concerned that Joe had sought her out. He must have gone to a lot of trouble too; she wasn't in the phone book. She couldn't think of one reason he should want to find her. People didn't trace people from newspaper pictures just to say "Howdy."

"Ellen? Who is it?"

Ellen groaned at the sound of Lettice's voice. There was no sense trying to explain this to her grandmother.

"Just an acquaintance," she called back to the dining room. "I'll be there in a moment, Grandmother."

She stepped outside and pulled the doors closed. The interruption had given her a moment to regain her equilibrium. But she sensed that under Joe's friendly exterior was a powerful cat stalking its increasingly mesmerized prey. The thought was scary.

Then it clicked in her head why a man she didn't know and hadn't encouraged would seek her out.

He was a fortune hunter.

Anger shot through her at the thought. It made sense. After all, she'd married one. And she'd attracted them before that. There must be a sign on her forehead that said Sucker. This one, though, was very bold for coming here out of the blue. His suave manners and pretty compliments were probably designed to smooth over the shock of his sudden appearance. She would bet what was left of her trust fund that his excuse for coming was that he had found a skate key and just knew it had to be hers.

"I would really like to talk to you about that day at the rink," he said. His smile was so casual on the surface. "Is there somewhere more private—"

"I'm very comfortable here," she interrupted, which wasn't exactly true. She felt warm, and she had no idea why. Then she realized her traitorous body was responding to the closeness of his. She edged away from him and focused on his face.

He was frowning at her. "Okay. Do you remember the man I pointed out to you when we were skating together?"

Bewildered by the totally unexpected question, she nodded.

"Did you happen to see him stop and talk to anybody?"

"I . . ." She paused. He asked the strangest questions for a fortune hunter. "Are you a policeman?"

It was his turn to look bewildered. "No."

"Then I don't think I should tell you."

"But . . . Why?"

"Because I don't know who you are." He started to speak, but she held up her hand. "I mean, I don't know you or anything about you or the man you're asking about. And you're not a policeman doing your job or anything. It's only common sense."

"Maybe I'm trying to give him his lottery winnings," Joe pointed out.

"They announce the winning numbers on TV," she said, setting her jaw. She vaguely remembered the man he was asking about standing with someone after Joe had made his exit. Still, it would be foolish to say anything. And this need for her "help" could be a ruse to somehow gain her confidence. She wasn't quite ready to let go of her fortune-hunter theory. She wasn't sure she should. "I can't help you."

He took a deep breath and stared hard at her, clearly becoming frustrated with her. "Look, it's all right. He's my cousin, Mario Penza. I'm the chief executive officer of Carlini Foods, and Mario works for me. I eat all my vegetables and think fairly clean thoughts, if you need a further recommendation. Believe me, I really am a good guy."

He seemed just as earnest and charming as he had been at the rink, and she could feel that invisible pull urging her to move closer to the heat and protection of him.

Ellen swallowed and forced the urge away. What he said he was and what he was could be two different things. She'd been fooled before. About time she started being overly cautious, she thought with satisfaction. Her grandmother would be proud.

She shook her head. "I'm sorry."

He made a face. Hunching his shoulders, he shoved his hands into his pants pockets. "I guess

I should feel complimented. Most people think I'm so upstanding that I'm dull."

The last thing he looked was dull. . . .

Suddenly, the polished brass doorknob was pulled from her hand. She whipped around as the door swung open to reveal her grandmother.

"Ellen, where are your manners?" Lettice asked reprovingly. "This is too long to be out on the step. Even if your friend can't stay, you could at least ask him into the house."

Ellen groaned loudly. "Grandmother, you don't understand—"

"I understand rudeness."

"Your granddaughter is being cautious," Joe said. "I'm Joe Carlini. Ellen and I have met only once before, when she rescued me at the roller skating rink."

"That's done it," Ellen muttered.

"Roller skating rink?" her grandmother repeated, her eyebrows shooting up in perfect, outraged arches.

Joe nodded innocently. Ellen closed her eyes in resignation.

"Yes," she heard him say. "She's very good on skates, but I'm sure you know that."

"I see."

Ellen opened her eyes as her grandmother turned to her.

"I thought we discussed this once before," Lettice said coldly.

The queen of England could take lessons in being regal from Lettice Kitteridge, Ellen thought, then shook her head. Really, this was ridiculous. Lettice had caught her coming home from a rink during a vacation from school when she was six-teen, and she'd been the victim of a "discussion" then. Sixteen, for heaven's sake! Anyway, she'd told herself enough times that she was a grown woman. Now she ought to start acting like one.

"We did discuss this before, Grandmother." She gazed steadily into the older woman's eyes. "Nearly fifteen years ago. I'm thirty now and answerable only to me."

Her grandmother drew herself up even straighter. "We will discuss this—"

"No. This is the end of the discussion."

Lettice gaped at her in astonishment. It wasn't surprising, Ellen admitted, as she took the oppor-tunity to brush past Joe and head for the garage around the left side of the mansion. Sometimes her grandmother took the term "grande dame" a little too seriously. Over her shoulder she added, "I've decided I need a dress for the dance, Grand-mother, so I'm going to Suki Rosen's now. I'll be home in time for a *pleasant* dinner. Good day, Joe."

That wasn't so bad, she decided as she made her escape. In fact, it was downright invigorating to stand up for herself.

"That was a very good speech," Joe said, catch-ing up with her.

She glanced over in surprise and was discon-certed to see him keeping pace with her.

"It was meant for you too," she said, and turned back again. She stared blankly at the blooming azaleas lining the walkway, trying to ignore him. It wasn't easy. Her hand brushed against his and hot fire burned its way to her shoulder before she could move away.

"I wish I could be nicer about this," he said, "but unfortunately I'm too desperate. All I need is a description, or even just that he was huddled with somebody. Anybody. It's extremely important."

He sounded more sincere than before. She forced herself not to feel guilty. "Then ask your cousin. If that's what he is."

"He is, but I don't think he would tell me if I asked him."

"Then I can't help you. Good day, Joe."

She hustled past him and ran to the garages. It wasn't until she was in the Audi passing both him and her grandmother that she allowed herself to sigh with relief. She acknowledged that she'd just gained a bit of self-respect.

And a little peace and quiet.

She thought he was a nut.

Of course, she would, Joe admitted dryly, as he sat in his large corner office of Carlini Foods later that afternoon. Every time she saw him, he was acting like one. He might be able to run a company, but he was lousy at the espionage business. He shouldn't complain about her reaction, anyway. After the way she had disappeared from the rink, his had been no better. He'd thought *she* was the person Mario was to meet. They had both conveniently disappeared while he'd been falling on his face. The theory made sense—until he'd seen her picture in the paper.

Ignoring the piles of paperwork cluttering his

huge, polished teak desk, he stared at the photograph. It made no sense for someone like Ellen Kitteridge to be involved in stealing Carlini Foods' most closely guarded secret. He doubted she'd do something for "kicks." She just didn't seem that way. After all, she had once been a princess, a job with no time for kicks, he was sure. Knowing she had been married to an Italian playboy prince was vaguely intimidating. He wasn't sure why, but it was. No wonder she had seemed familiar, though. She had been in the news enough times. More than her fair share, really.

The death of her child had been international front-page headlines. How, he wondered in awe and sympathy, had she survived that?

After discovering who she was, he should have realized she'd been guarding her privacy. If he had told her the truth about Mario right away, maybe she would have been more willing to talk, he decided belatedly. Instead, he'd been vague because of his own caution, and then there hadn't been an opportunity to correct the matter. Witnessing the discussion between her and her grandmother, he had finally known why she had left the rink without a good-bye. She skated on the sly.

Joe grinned. It was intriguing to know the elegant jet-setter liked something as simple as roller skating. Her body movements were naturally graceful, with a sexiness that left him breathless. Unfortunately, he'd been the cause of embarrassment for her, and he doubted if she appreciated it. He certainly wouldn't if the situation had been reversed.

Still, she was his only hope.

"Dammit," Joe cursed out loud, as a wave of guilt at using Ellen washed through him. But he hadn't spent years building Carlini Foods to where it was to have some punk like Mario pull it down. He knew he couldn't do anything until he had absolute proof of Mario's treachery. As much as he hated to admit it, a roller skating rink hadn't been such a crazy choice for a secret meeting. The place had the friendliness of a neighborhood stoop and the anonymity of a subway station. Two people could meet and chat without anyone thinking it odd. . . .

But he'd violated the anonymity part with Ellen.

He had to fix that, and very soon. Ellen Kitteridge was surprising and puzzling, he mused. On the outside she was serene and poised. Yet he had glimpsed yet again today the fire inside her.

He had to see her again. He had to prove to her that he wasn't a nut. He also needed an edge with Mario, and he had a feeling she could provide it.

Ellen Kitteridge gave him an edge all right, Joe thought, smiling.

And in more ways than one.

One week later, Ellen stood on the orchestra stage in front of hundreds of people at the Four Seasons Hotel and smiled stiffly at Joe Carlini. The heat of anger and embarrassment flushed her cheeks as she accepted the oversized check from him.

"As chief executive officer of Carlini Foods," he announced into the microphone, "I am pleased to make this donation to Graduate Hospital."

"On behalf of the Graduate Hospital Fund-raising Committee, I thank you very much," she said, forcing herself to offer her hand for the traditional handshake. Her fury and humiliation deepened as she thought of her "fortune-hunter" theory.

His strong fingers closed around hers, and the now familiar reaction to him burned through her body. Camera flashes popped and applause filled the room.

"You stinker," Ellen added succinctly through the din.

His jaw dropped in astonishment. "What?"

"You heard me." She pulled her hand away and, turning around, walked briskly off the stage.

Lettice was waiting at the front of the stairs. "Very nicely done."

Ellen shoved the check into her grandmother's hands. "Very forcibly done, you mean."

Lettice shrugged. "He insisted on you accepting it. It's a very sizable and much needed check. He seems nice enough—no visible warts at any rate. What else could we do without making a fuss?"

"That's the first rule of the Kitteridges, isn't it?" Ellen said, her voice as dry as the Gobi desert. "Never make a fuss when being humiliated in front of everyone."

She walked away, leaving her grandmother staring after her.

"Is the check too small?" Joe asked as he appeared alongside her.

"No, and you damn well know it," she said, giving him an angry glance. To her disbelief, her brain registered how attractively his tuxedo fit his leanly muscled frame. The music began again, and she continued along the edge of the dance floor, determined to collect her things and get to her car as fast as she could. She wanted . . . needed to get away from him.

"Anybody ever tell you you're very emotional?" he asked.

She whirled around on him, oblivious to witnesses. "I'm not emotional!"

"Could have fooled me," he said, looking pointedly at the people surrounding them.

"Right." She took his elbow and dragged him onto the dance floor. As he put his arm around her back, she kept a foot of space between them. She willed herself to ignore the hot rush that thundered through her body at his touch. His eyes held a knowing look. She could ignore that too. Smiling sweetly as they began to dance, she added, "Please excuse me if I step on your toes. I plan to frequently."

"And I just gave you a check."

"To prove you were exactly who you said you were. But did you have to do it so publicly? A letter on company stationery or a newspaper article with your picture or even a case of romano cheese would have done just as well." She stared up at him, resisting the urge to smack his handsome face. "But you insisted on giving the check here at the dance and only to me. I'm not even a member of the committee! And I certainly don't want my picture in the paper, and now it will be. And I don't want people talking about me, and now they are. I've had enough of that to last a lifetime."

He gazed at her for a long moment, then shook

his head. "When I blow it, I do a bang-up job. Look, Ellen, I'm really sorry. I honestly thought you would appreciate the donation and realize I'm not a nut."

"You'll have a hard time proving it by me." She sighed in resignation. "I suppose, though, it isn't entirely your fault. I'm not sure why I should suppose that, but I do."

"I promise I'm not crazy, and I don't have 'things' about people, so do you think you can stretch your imagination just a little further and help me?" he asked, swinging her around in time to the music.

"I guess I better." She smiled slightly. "Lord knows what you'll do next time."

"I'm a desperate man," he agreed.

She admitted that he was a man, at least. Very much one. His tuxedo jacket fit his broad shoulders perfectly and emphasized his lean waist and hips. Even with the space between them, she could feel the heat from his body. Her own body was responding with the growing urge to move closer, to touch hip to hip, breast to chest. . . .

"I'm better off the skates," he said in a low voice.

She swallowed. "It just takes some practice."

His gaze lowered, taking in her dress. The long bodice of burgundy lace clung to her breasts and hips, and the calf-length cream taffeta skirt was tucked up on one side by a cluster of burgundy roses. "You're very beautiful in that dress. At first I thought I was seeing more than I should."

"It's an illusion," she murmured, her resistance melting at his intimate tone.

Words seemed inappropriate after that. He pulled her closer, until her breasts were touching his chest. Her nipples began to throb at the feel of a hard, muscular chest. His thighs brushed hers, rubbing her skirt against her sheer silk stockings. Her veins were filled with hot syrup. . . .

She realized how much danger she was in and immediately stepped out of his arms. "I have to go home now."

"I'll walk you to your car," he volunteered.

"I'm fine."

He took her arm and steered her off the dance floor. "I'll walk you. Besides, you've just agreed to help me, and we need to discuss that."

His expression dared her to argue with him. She didn't, knowing it would be futile. Anyway, she thought in disgust, if she argued with him, the newspaper columnist here tonight would probably print it word for word.

They were silent until they were outside and the doorman had called for her car. Joe guided her away into the shadows for a little privacy while they waited. She pulled her coat tighter around her body, grateful for the cool air. It would keep her head clear, and her internal temperature down.

"How am I supposed to help you?" she asked briskly.

"Let me explain my problem first," he said, his own voice businesslike. "Carlini Foods is a family-owned and run business, and although we went national three years ago, we haven't changed much from when my great-grandfather started the company. Mario, the guy from the rink, really is my cousin. He was hired a few years ago and as a family member was put in a position of some trust. But very reluctantly. He's always been a little too wild. I have good reason to suspect he's trying to sell our tomato-sauce recipe."

Ellen froze. "Did you say sauce?"

Joe nodded. "Yes. Mama Carlini's Homestyle Italian Sauce, to be exact."

She felt as if the shadows were closing in on her. "I don't believe it. You pester and humiliate me for a sauce recipe?"

Joe snorted. "I didn't pester, and I said I was sorry. Ellen, it's a sauce recipe that's worth millions."

She gasped. "Of *dollars*?"

"Food is big business. Our sauce has a quarter of the national market, and it's the cornerstone of the company. As I said, Mario was given some trust, and he has access to a quarter of the sauce processing, and therefore a quarter of the recipe itself. Three other family members each have another quarter. Only my father, as past CEO, and myself know the entire recipe and processing. And there's just one written copy that is kept in my office safe. We're tighter than the Coca-Cola people."

"I would guess so," Ellen murmured, awed by all the secrecy for a sauce recipe.

Joe let out a long breath. "At least I thought we were secure, until I overheard a piece of Mario's phone conversation with someone last week. He offered to sell the recipe. I'm damned if I know how he got it, but I'm not surprised he'd sell it. He always needs money, more than his salary and stock dividends pay. To say he likes his lifestyle expensive is an understatement. And he's found out borrowing money from the company is impossible. If he manages to sell the recipe to a big food conglomerate, they could produce the sauce more cheaply, and that would put us out of business very quickly. I'm telling you more than I've told my own father, but I have to stop Mario."

"Can't you just fire him?" she asked. "Surely you have cause."

"I have to have solid proof. That's the problem with a family business. You can't fire someone on suspicion. Can you tell me anything you might have noticed about him that day? If he talked to anyone, handed something to anyone?"

Millions of dollars, she thought absently, as she realized what her excessive caution might have caused. Joe was trying to save his family from ruin, and she had nearly blocked him. She concentrated on that morning at the rink. "I did see him talking to a man when I was getting my skates off. I remember them because, besides me, they were the only ones who weren't at least looking toward your . . . exit."

He made a face. "Just talking? He didn't give him anything?"

"Well, no, not that I could see."

"And the man. Can you describe him?"

"Dark hair, I think." She shrugged helplessly. "Very average. I mean, nothing stood out about him. I feel foolish about being so stubborn the other day. Telling it now, there really isn't anything even a nut could use."

Joe chuckled. "Actually, more than you think. At least he met with somebody while I was occupied."

She giggled, thinking of how he had flown out

the door with the greatest of ease. "If I had known there would be a pop quiz, I would have studied harder."

"Would you know the other man if you saw him again?"

"I suppose," she began, unsure. "I think so."

He smiled. "If I find out my cousin is meeting someone again, would you be willing to help me one more time?"

She wanted desperately to say no. Joe Carlini was dangerous to her. She could feel it with her every helpless response to him. But she just couldn't shake the idea that she might be contributing to the theft of millions of dollars if she didn't.

"I guess I owe you something," she finally said, grinning at him.

"I promise to make it worth your while," he said.

His head bent suddenly, and he captured her mouth in a kiss, taking her by complete surprise. It started out as a kiss of gratitude, but quickly changed to one that sent pleasure and alarm spreading through her body. The conflicting emotions swirled through her senses with equal intensity, stilling any protest.

His kiss was like fire, she thought dimly. Hot and sweet and drugging all at the same time. She found herself opening her mouth to his, even as her arms crept around his shoulders. Her hands delighted in the feel of strong muscles beneath the expensive material. Her tongue dueled with his until the air was roaring in her ears. It wasn't supposed to be like this, she thought. Not . . . perfection.

Suddenly he lifted his head. "Your car's here, Ellen."

His matter-of-fact words halted the wild spinning, and she crashed back to earth.

She straightened, opening her mouth to tell him that couldn't happen again.

He set his finger against her lips, stopping her before she started her lecture. "Don't. It was just a kiss."

She stared at him. If that was just a kiss, then he'd obviously never heard of a volcano. She certainly felt like one about to erupt. Dammit, why had she ever agreed to help him? She prayed he never heard another thing about his cousin.

She fought the urge to throw herself back into his arms when he took her elbow to escort her to her car. She decided Ellen Kitteridge was synonymous with "Big Dummy." She didn't know whether to run away in fear or scream in frustration.

Instead, she got in her car and drove home.

Three

"Atlantic City!"

Ellen gasped into the telephone. It was only noon on the day after the dance, and Joe expected her just to hop into the car and go to Atlantic City with him? He *was* crazy. And she must have been insane to have agreed to help him.

"I've discovered Mario is going down to the Palace tonight," he said. "He gambles there, but I have a feeling it's for more than—"

"Joe," she interrupted, trying to get as much steel as possible into her voice, "I know I said I would help you if I could, but I cannot go to Atlantic City with you!"

"It's just for an evening, Ellen. You might catch a glimpse of the person Mario was with at the rink."

She smiled thinly. "Now I've been wondering how that would help. After all, even if it was the same person, how could you find out who he is?"

"You'd be surprised," Joe said, patience clear in his voice. "If I could get a look at him, I might be able to trace him. I know you're not thrilled about this. . . ."

That was an understatement if she had ever heard one.

". . . but I promise to be a good boy and to spot you twenty dollars for the slot machines."

She chuckled. Still, the Palace was a hotel . . . with rooms . . . and they would be together. . . .

"Does it have to be Atlantic City? I mean, can't we wait until he goes to the rink again?"

"You just want to see me fall flat on my face, don't you?"

"It's tempting."

"Look, Atlantic City is only a couple of hours away. You'll have a nice evening of dinner and gambling, with some looking around in between."

She hesitated. She had called her lawyer for some background on Joe Carlini. After all, she had reasoned, she had a right to know. But she had been surprised at the sudden enthusiasm from her normally unflappable counselor. It seemed that Joe had taken Carlini Foods, a thriving regional company, and made it national three years ago when he had become CEO. The company had already acquired five percent of the overall national market, which was evidently some kind of food miracle, and the sauce in question had over twenty percent of the tomato-sauce market. Joe had also brought out a line of gourmet Italian sauces and pasta that had found markets in specialty stores. He was credited with building up

Carlini Foods until it was practically a blue-chip investment.

No wonder he was desperate to keep all that safe.

"Ell?"

She swallowed at the way he had shortened her name. It held an intimacy that she'd never heard before—from anyone.

"All right," she finally said. "But just an evening in Atlantic City. If your cousin's planning to leave from there for New York or Boston or anywhere else north, south, east, or west, you are on your own. Agreed?"

"Agreed. I'll pick you up about two."

"Two! But that's the middle of the afternoon!"

"It takes a couple of hours to get there, and I think it would be better if we were already there and settled in when he arrived."

She gripped the phone tightly. Unfortunately, his plan made sense. "Fine. Two."

"Not only are you beautiful, but you're a great human being, Ellen."

"And you," she said dryly, "are a great soft-soaper, Mr. Carlini."

"I'm never soft when I'm around you. I'll see you in a couple of hours."

He hung up before she could get her mouth open to say anything, including "good-bye."

"Great," she muttered, setting the receiver down in its cradle. She wondered if she had imagined that sudden intimate turn to his voice—or the way he seemed to be talking about something entirely different than she.

If she wasn't imagining things, then she would

have to correct any mistaken impression he might have about her. Okay, so his mouth had created a firestorm in her, and his arms had felt so right around her. She was an adult who could control her reactions. She'd help him this one time, and that was it.

No more Ms. Nice Guy, Ellen sternly told herself. She'd been Ms. Nice Guy in Europe. She decided she'd better tell her grandmother about her "date" this evening.

Now that, she thought, groaning silently, would be interesting.

As he steered his Mercedes through the heavy afternoon traffic on the Atlantic City expressway, Joe sneaked yet another glance at the woman sitting in the passenger seat.

Ellen Kitteridge looked as if she were made for his car. She had an elegance that suited the butter-rich tan leather interior. She wore a cream silk shirt and matching skirt. Her only jewelry was gold button earrings and a single, delicate gold chain nestled under the shirt's lapels. Yet he could easily believe she was once a princess.

"When I was a kid," he said, wanting to dispel the tense silence between them, "we always used to go down the shore. Mostly to Wildwood. What about you?"

"Mostly to Ocean City."

It figured, he thought. Ocean City was the premier shore point on the Jersey coast.

Suddenly she chuckled. "You said 'down the shore.' That's a local term. Everywhere else people say, 'We're going to the beach or *to* the shore,' but not 'down the shore.' "

"How do you know that?" he asked.

"I studied modern language at college." She shook her head and laughed. "There's a real call for that with the job recruiters. I also have an appreciation for things Philadelphian."

He nodded, while thinking that her appreciation certainly hadn't included Philadelphian men. Nope, she had had to marry a prince from northern Italy, when there were plenty of Italians right here at home. *Philadelphian* Italians.

"I asked around about you," she said. "I hope you don't mind."

"It all depends on what was said," he answered, giving her a smile.

She smiled back. "That Carlini Foods was smart to make you CEO."

"Too bad they can't see me now," he quipped.

She laughed. "Does anyone know about your penchant for playing *I Spy*?"

"No, I'm happy to say. So who do you want to be? Alexander Scott or Kelly Robinson?"

"Scotty."

"Very smart. He had all the great lines, and he went on to be Bill Cosby. That leaves me as Kelly." He paused for a minute. "I wouldn't have thought you knew about that show."

"Even the Kitteridges have been known to watch TV upon occasion," she said dryly. "Anyway, it's still an extremely popular show in Europe. And very American. I was desperate for things American."

"Each country has a different mind-set," Joe said, thinking of his own experiences traveling in

Europe. When she didn't say anything more, he decided to prod her. "Was it that tough being a princess?"

She shrugged. "I was supposed to be the next Grace Kelly. You know, the little Philadelphia girl who married the prince of her dreams. Well, after I met Florian, my . . . husband, I discovered I literally couldn't breathe without making all the tabloids. And Florian had the idea that he was the playboy prince of Lombardy. The problem was, he forgot to tell me that before the wedding. He also forgot to tell me that he needed my money for his crumbling estates in northern Italy. He was too busy skiing to run them properly."

"One of those, eh?" Although he felt bad for her, Joe had to admit to himself a certain satisfaction knowing that the prince was a bastard underneath.

She nodded. "One of those. And the family mansion outside Parma was falling down faster than it could be fixed. Truthfully, I'm to blame, too, since I didn't want to notice. Not really. Anyway, he liked to flaunt conventions, to put it mildly, and his countrymen loved him for it. I wound up taking over a lot of his responsibilities. Of course, Florian's mother and aunts couldn't handle all the duties. I was kind of like the booby prize. And then . . ."

Her voice trailed away. Joe glanced at her. Her jaw was set, so he finished the sentence for her, to get it out in the open. "And then your son died."

"Drowned," she said, with a poignant catch in her voice. She stared down at her hands. "Paulo fell into the canal when only I was with him. He was pulled under some docked boats by the strong current. He couldn't surface, and I dived . . . I couldn't find him." She paused for a long moment. "He was four."

"I admire you," he said quietly, knowing her husband had blamed her in every newspaper he could for the accident. He reached over to cover the too-tightly clenched hands in her lap with his own. She started, gazing at him suddenly with wide eyes, and he added, "Despite the tremendous unfairness, you never once gave a show for the public."

He had taken her hands only to give her support, yet suddenly and uncontrollably the support changed to something more primitive at the contact of skin to skin. He felt the blood curling thickly through him, and he could feel the same in her. His breath was rasping in his throat. Where her fingers had been cold at first, they now were warm—almost hot. And her thighs brushed restlessly, enticingly, against his hand.

She turned, unclasping her hands in such a way that his slid naturally off her lap. He took the wheel again, without comment. Her breathing was audible, but her attempt at a nonchalant shrug wasn't far off the mark as she picked up the conversation again. "Now all I want is a little peace and quiet. And privacy."

"For roller skating."

She made a face at him, and he smiled. But he had heard a fierce determination in her voice when she had spoken of peace and privacy. It bothered him, as if she were shutting out the world quietly but surely. She was beautiful, he thought, poised and serene. And very vulnerable; she always would be. And she had a dry sense of humor. He hadn't expected that. He couldn't allow someone like her to lock herself away.

"Now that I've told my dismal tale of woe that everybody already knows," she said, "what about yours?"

He shrugged. "There's nothing to tell."

"Joe, I don't even know where you live or whether you're married."

"What!" he exclaimed. "You didn't get that in your report?"

"Nope, except that you seem married to Carlini Foods."

"Sometimes I think that's too true." He glanced at her. She was looking at him expectantly. "Okay. We live in Wynnewood—"

"You really are married!"

He grinned. "Scared ya, didn't I? Actually, I have apartments at the family home. Now that my dad is retired, my parents spend about ten months out of the year traveling. It was convenient to be close to my father when I was learning the business. Then I never seemed to find the time to move, and now I'm there by myself for most of the year."

Ellen shrugged. "Where I come from, people don't buy their estates, they inherit them. So you're not married."

"Not to a woman, anyway," he said, tacitly acknowledging her comment about his job. "Was once."

"Divorce?"

He shook his head.

"I'm sorry, Joe," she said sincerely.

He cleared his throat. "To tell you the truth, I always feel a little guilty when someone says that. I married young, at twenty, against everybody's advice. Gina was helpless and clinging . . . innocent, I guess. At first I was flattered that she needed me so much, and then I felt smothered by it. She died in a car accident nearly a year later. Being older and wiser now, I realize that I got married more out of a need for rebellion than for love. I—I was glad I didn't have to hurt her. Hell of a thing to say, isn't it?"

Ellen frowned. "No . . . not really. You've just recognized that the marriage wouldn't have worked out. You shouldn't feel guilty about that."

"You're probably right," he said. Still, he never had been able to shake a vague feeling of guilt. Nor had he ever told anyone about it. He'd never had the urge to, before now. Probably not a wise urge, he thought. He'd been having quite a few unwise urges around Ellen. It was a relief to know that she understood.

He couldn't imagine her clinging and dependent. She stood alone. A little too alone to suit him.

They passed a huge, glittering billboard that advertised the Palace Casino. The shaft of the sign's arrow bore the legend: 10 miles.

"Not too much longer till your first assignment, Scotty," Joe said, glancing over at her.

"As long as it's my last," she replied in the sweetest of voices.

He studied the slender line of her throat, her

full breasts, and the faint V of her thighs under her skirt. He shifted his gaze back to the road and smiled to himself.

It wouldn't be the last time, if he had something to say about it.

Ellen was staring at his mouth, feeling again the firmness of his lips against hers, their tongues dueling in a kiss of fire. . . .

"See him?" Joe asked.

Startled from her reverie, she dutifully dragged her gaze away from his mouth and shook her head. She edged away from him and looked down into the "pit" from their spot at the lobby railing. "No. Still no sign of your cousin."

It was futile, she thought. The casino was enormous, with more twists and dead ends than an eighteenth-century garden maze. People milled about continually as the din of voices, the chink of coins, and the bing of slot machines filled the air. She and Joe had been there for six hours and still hadn't spotted Mario. The man could have met two hundred people by this time, she figured, and they wouldn't know it.

Joe muttered a curse of frustration.

"Sorry," he apologized.

She smiled. "Actually, I was thinking the same thing." Still, the bustle and excitement here was very different from European casinos, and she privately reveled in it. "It's ten o'clock, Joe. We've wandered around and placed ourselves in strategic locations in order to watch the rooms. But there are mobs of people here tonight, and unfortunately my eyes keep wandering to the glitzy chandeliers, gold wallpaper, and floor-length mirrors. This place is more opulent than Versailles. And you and I have lost each other twice so far, so it's not surprising that we can't find Mario. Any suggestions?"

"Other than paging him," Joe said in disgust, "I'm out of ideas."

Ellen looked around the casino again. She wished her commitment to Joe was over. She was finding it all too easy to be around him, and he was much too attractive to suit her. She had decided long ago that if she was ever going to be interested in a man again, he would have to be short and pale. Not tall, not bronzed, and definitely not good-looking. Joe was all three and then some. He could turn her to jelly with the slightest touch. The more she was in his company, the more she was attracted to him. Twice she had been horrified to find herself gazing at his mouth, wondering what it would be like to kiss him again. And she was already telling him things she had never told anybody before. He was dangerous, very dangerous to her barely regained sanity. She didn't need this now. All she wanted to do was go home. Even a lecture from her grandmother was better than this.

He leaned forward, his arm brushing hers as he peered at the crowd. Her blood leaped in her veins. She forced herself not to show it and turned her mind back to the problem at hand.

"I wish we could have looked in the private gambling rooms," she said, her voice only a little shaky. "But we can't without him spotting us instantly."

Joe shrugged. "I was just thinking that any of the regular hotel rooms upstairs could be used for private games. We could hardly watch them."

Ellen straightened as his earlier words came back to her. "Why don't we page him?"

"Ell, don't be facetious—"

"I'm serious. If he answers, then we know he's here for sure, and if he doesn't, then either he didn't come, or else he's somewhere where he can't hear it, like a private room, and we can forget it and go home." She was panting by the time she finished her rush of words. "Anyway, what have we got to lose?"

"I must be crazy," he muttered, gazing around the crowded casino.

"We already know that." She took his arm and steered him away from the railing. Why was it, she wondered, that when she was prepared for physical contact, she could handle it? She decided, for the moment, to concentrate on her idea. If it didn't work, she was afraid they'd be stuck here for the night, and that didn't bear thinking about. "Come on. There's a bank of telephones at the far wall. They're the only ones I've seen so far, so if he's anywhere in the casino, he's sure to come here."

"You like this," Joe said.

She grinned. "It beats playing the slots until we're both out of quarters."

"We *are* out of quarters."

"See?"

When they reached the house telephones, Ellen

immediately went to one near the end, away from several people who were talking into others. Clearly the phones were popular tonight.

"I'll make the call," she said, while scanning the instructions for use that were pasted on the booth's wall. "You find a place where you can watch the phones as discreetly as possible. Oh! I know he's not a Carlini, but I forget what he is."

"Penza." Joe took her arm and turned her to face him. "You're having fun," he said, his gaze steady on hers.

"Might as well," she joked lamely, an odd feeling sizzling along her nerve endings at his closeness. "We're not making any progress in the spy business."

"I didn't expect you to be like this, you know."

"How did you expect me to be?" she asked. His cologne was subtle and very masculine, not at all overpowering, and it sent her senses spinning.

"I don't know," he murmured. "But not like this."

He lowered his head and touched her mouth briefly with his. It was enough to feel the firm heat of his lips and the way they fit perfectly to hers. The sensations intensified so fast that it scared and enticed her at the same time.

He lifted his head and stared at her for a long moment. Then he smiled. "Keep kissing me like that, and we'll both be in trouble. Have fun. I'll go play Agent Thirteen."

Who, Ellen wondered dimly as she watched him go, was Agent Thirteen?

At last, she turned back to the phone. Following the directions, she asked the operator for the page and waited for results. She had her back toward the other phones in case Mario should recognize her from the rink. But she desperately wanted to turn around . . .

"Mario Penza here."

She nearly dropped the phone in her astonishment. *Son-of-a-gun,* she thought, *it worked.*

"Ah . . . yes . . . Mr. Penza," she said, talking through her nose to disguise her voice. "This is the hotel manager's office, and we're having a small problem with room reservations. Have you taken a room here tonight, sir?"

"No, I haven't."

"Oh, dear. Well, thank you for your help. Please enjoy the casino tonight, Mr. Penza."

She pushed the cutoff button down while still holding the receiver to her ear. Grinning, she sighed with relief and decided that Joe was right. She was having fun.

He materialized in front of her, whispering, "Hang it up, Ell, and come on!"

She shoved the receiver back onto its hook, even as Joe took hold of her elbow. She almost had to run to keep up with his long stride.

"I can't believe it worked," he said.

"People will always answer a page," she said breathlessly, as they weaved through the crowds of gamblers. Excitement and anxiety waged war inside her. And something more, for she was all too aware of Joe's touch on her elbow. She went on. "It's curiosity combined with the concern that it might actually be important. Will you slow down! We're practically on top of him."

"I literally can't afford to lose him."

She was tempted to remind him that Mario

might lead them on a wild-goose chase if he noticed them, but she didn't. She supposed she ought to keep her comments to herself. After all, this was Joe's problem and her little bit to help him was almost over. One point of the finger was all that was left to be done. Then she'd be back to home and bed—and peace and quiet.

It sounded dull.

Ellen set her jaw. She wanted privacy, and if it meant being a little dull, then she could certainly live with that. And she would make sure Joe understood that too. When she had a moment to tell him.

They rounded the end of a long line of slot machines just in time to see Mario walk into the lounge. He held his head up and his shoulders square. Although Joe's cousin wasn't very tall, it would be hard to miss the curly, nearly black, hair cut precisely to the point where it just grazed his shirt collar.

"Do you suppose he's been in here all the time?" Joe asked in a low voice.

"We must have checked here every fifteen minutes!" Ellen said in disbelief. "We couldn't have missed him."

"True." Joe stopped on the threshold and stared into the dimly lit room. "I don't see him. Do you?"

She peered inside. Except for the occupants of the first few tables, she could see only shadows and silhouettes. "No. The light's bad."

"We'll have to go in."

"But—"

That was as far as her protest got. He tightened his grip on her elbow and pulled her into the lounge. When they were finally perched on stools at the bar, she was breathless as much from his touch as from his speed. Her eyes slowly adjusted to the low lighting. Fortunately, the lounge was between floor shows, so she wasn't distracted by a bright stage. She glanced around again.

"There," she said quietly, nodding toward a back booth. Sitting directly under the booth's yellow light was Mario. He was talking intently to someone else in the booth.

Joe turned casually, leaning his elbow on the bar. "I see him."

The man Mario was talking with leaned forward into the light. . . .

"I don't think it's the same man," Ellen said, peering intently. "His profile is too . . . defined. Unfortunately. It's not the same person from the rink, Joe."

"I know."

"You do?" She turned to look at him and was even more surprised to see his features hard with anger. "You know him?"

He nodded. "All too well. It's my uncle Thomas."

Ellen glanced back at the two men. "Not his father, I take it."

Joe smiled grimly at her. "You take it right. Uncle Thomas is the last person I'd expect Mario to be with. I doubt Mario has bothered to say more than hello to Thomas in years. But here they both are, and cozy too. I don't understand this. I thought he was selling the recipe at the rink."

"But what does your uncle have to do with any of that?" Ellen asked.

"Too much. Remember I told you Mario has, by right of his position, access to a quarter of the recipe?"

She nodded.

"Uncle Thomas has one quarter of the recipe. If what's going on is what I think is going on, Mario is about to have access to *two* quarters of the recipe. Another cousin and my sister hold the other two. I wonder now if the rink meeting was to arrange things with a buyer before he stole the recipe. Maybe he doesn't actually have it yet. Dammit! Don't tell me I have to watch all of them!"

Ellen groaned. It was easy to guess whom he was going to ask to help him.

Four

Panic, Joe admitted, was probably in order. Thomas Carlini was gregarious and generous and completely without guile. While the older man would guard his part of the recipe from outsiders with his life, he was capable of giving it away to another family member—if Mario's need was "innocent." And Mario knew it.

Joe had been puzzling about how Mario could have acquired the recipe. The only people who had the entire thing were Joe himself, his father, the senior lawyer, whose honesty would have made Diogenes ecstatic, and the safe. Mario had to be assembling the four parts. The situation was not as far along as he had feared. His other cousin, Jamie, and his own sister, Carol, had the other two quarters of the recipe. Ten minutes ago, he had complete faith in them. Now he wasn't quite so sure. But even if Mario acquired only Thomas's quarter, that in itself could be disastrous. In the same way an anthropologist could rebuild a man from an arm bone, someone could rebuild the recipe from just a part of it. They might not get it precisely right, but they could get a fair clone.

Joe's head was spinning, and he felt as if he were playing a chess game with someone who was changing the rules every second move. He decided that he'd make a few rules of his own before it was over. He also decided this was not the time to be peering out from behind palm trees.

"Joe!" Ellen whispered fiercely as he took her hand and headed straight for the booth cradling his relatives. "Wait! What are you doing, and let me in on it!"

"Just follow my lead," he said. Her hand was warm in his, and he smiled to himself, although he knew this was hardly the moment for one of Ellen's distractions.

"It figures," she muttered loud enough for him to hear. "In *I Spy*, Robinson was always the impulsive one."

He grinned over his shoulder at her. She was right. He had no idea what he was going to do. He only knew he had to do something. "Just remember Scotty's job was to rescue Robinson."

They reached the booth before she could reply. The gods were with him, Joe thought, then tried to look startled and pleased as the two men glanced up.

"Thomas! And Mario!" he exclaimed cheerfully, watching his uncle smile back in innocent delight. Mario's initial shock was instantly covered by a smile that didn't reach the cold, narrowed eyes. Both men rose to their feet as Joe added,

"We came down to do a little gambling, but I didn't know you two were going to be here tonight too. And together."

"Joey!" Thomas said. Joe ignored the snort of feminine amusement at his uncle's use of the boyhood nickname. Thomas shook his hand, saying, "This is a wonderful surprise. Are you here for Sinatra too?"

"Sinatra?"

Thomas nodded.

Joe smiled sourly. Thomas loved Frank Sinatra. Mario was pushing all the right buttons. "We're here for the gambling."

"You're missing a great show then. Mario got some tickets from somewhere—I don't ask—for this private late show Sinatra's giving tonight, and he's treating his uncle Thomas instead of some pretty girl, bless him." Thomas looked at Ellen and smiled. "I see you have a pretty girl with you, Joey. A very pretty girl. Come and join us for a little while. Mario won't mind my asking. We're all family."

Joe pulled Ellen closer, putting his arm around her waist. His mind was racing with the twin thoughts of keeping Thomas from trouble and watching his own back at the same time, but it was instantly sidetracked by the soft curve of Ellen's waist and the subtle wave of heat that threatened to send his senses into oblivion. She stiffened at the contact, and he realized she was as affected as he.

"This is Ellen Kitteridge," he said, keeping his response to her at a minimum. "Ell, my uncle, Thomas Carlini, and my cousin, Mario Penza."

Ellen's smile was serene as she shook hands with both men. Joe wondered what Mario thought at seeing the woman from the skating rink with him again. Whatever he thought, it didn't show on his face.

"Do we have a few minutes, Ell?" he asked her, deferring to his "date" as any gentleman would.

Her smile never faltered. "I think so."

Joe decided he never wanted to play poker with her. No one would ever know if she held a royal flush or a pair of deuces.

"Wonderful!" Thomas exclaimed.

They ordered drinks and settled into the booth, with Ellen between him and Thomas. The long, lush line of her thigh brushed his, sending primitive signals coursing through him. Ellen jerked as if he'd run his hand along her leg. He wanted to. Badly. But he had a recipe to save. He felt caught between heaven and hell.

Deciding to take care of the hell first, he asked, "Well, Mario, how did you manage to get tickets for Sinatra? I heard the regular shows were sold out within hours of being booked."

"It's all in who you know," Mario said, shrugging.

"And you actually know someone. I'll keep it in mind next time I need hard-to-get tickets."

Mario glared at him, knowing he was being baited.

"I didn't realize you were a Sinatra fan, Mario," Joe went on, smiling. "I would have thought Sting was more your style."

"Who?" Uncle Thomas asked.

Mario shrugged again. "I wanted to treat Uncle Thomas."

Joe raised his right hand and vowed, "I promise not to tell your parents about your 'hot' date tonight. If I remember rightly, they like Sinatra too."

Mario's expressionless face could have been made from stone, Joe thought, knowing full well he had just hit the mark.

Thomas chuckled, then turned to Ellen. "Mary, Mario's mother, is a bigger fan than I am. And we're talking big!"

Everyone laughed.

Suddenly Thomas frowned. "Mary *is* a bigger fan. And she was just saying last week that she wished—"

Mario brought his hands together in a loud clap. "So, Joe, tell us about this beautiful new lady of yours. Have we met before, Ellen? You look very familiar."

Joe flinched at this sudden turn of the conversation. He had planted a little seed with Uncle Thomas that he expected, or more precisely hoped, would now niggle at the man. Thomas might just realize that he was being singled out in a big way by a nephew who had barely acknowledged him before. That Mario would attempt a diversion at this point wasn't surprising, but the direction of that diversion was. Joe didn't like it in the least that his cousin was focusing on Ellen.

She smiled demurely. "We haven't met before."

"Are you sure? But . . . Kitteridge . . . why is that name so familiar?" Mario mused aloud, the malicious glint in his eyes all too clear.

Joe could see his uncle frowning now for a different reason. The diversion was clearly working, but that was the least of Joe's worries. Clearly,

Mario was about to bring up Ellen's infamous background, possibly even the tragedy with her son. Red-hot anger shot through him at the thought of any embarrassment his cousin might cause Ellen. He'd take Mario by the throat to stop him, if he had to.

But Ellen was speaking already, calm and outwardly unflappable. "Kitteridges have been around Philadelphia for about two hundred and fifty years. Everybody knows us. My family does a lot of charity work, and several Kitteridges are in local politics. In fact, my father's cousin, Talman, is a rather flamboyant city councilman at large. He's always in the newspapers as an opponent of the current administration. It never seems to matter whose administration it is."

Uncle Thomas slapped the table. "Of course! Talman Kitteridge. He's run unsuccessfully for mayor five times."

"Six, actually," Ellen said, laughing. "The family joke is that nobody would be more shocked than Talman if he ever did win."

Joe hid a smile as she and Thomas launched into a discussion of her relative's antics. She had effectively cut off Mario's attempt to bring up her own past. He couldn't pursue the subject now, without looking as if he were deliberately trying to embarrass her. Joe gazed at her with frank admiration, at first for her adept turn of the conversation, and then just because she was Ellen. Her face was glowing and animated, and he knew it was partly because she was caught up in her role as spy. The other part he hoped had something to do with being with him. . . .

"She's delightful, Joey," Uncle Thomas pronounced with great satisfaction a few minutes later.

"Yes, I know." Joe smiled and took her hand under the table. He wasn't surprised by the jolt of electricity that passed through him. Ellen didn't flinch. Outwardly. After a decent moment, though, she deftly pulled her hand from his and began to fiddle with her glass.

Mario made a show of glancing at his watch. "We're going to have to go, Uncle Thomas."

Thomas nodded. "Sure. In a way it's a shame to go now. We were having such a nice talk with Joey and Ellen."

Ellen patted the older man's hand. "What a polite thing to say, and you're not fooling either of us with it. Go and enjoy the show, Thomas."

He grinned unabashedly at her.

"Yes, you lucky dog," Joe added, smiling at his uncle. "Besides, Mario would be mad as hell if you skipped the show, after all the trouble he went to for the tickets. I'm not surprised, though. After all, you're my favorite uncle, too."

"And mine, of course," Mario chimed in.

But it didn't ring true, and from Thomas's puzzled frown Joe knew his uncle was having doubts on the subject. He felt Thomas would be just a little suspicious and untrusting of Mario now. Enough to make the man stop and think about anything out of the ordinary before acting. Still, he would have to have a further chat with his uncle later to emphasize the point.

He imagined that Mario was none too happy with him at the moment. It was the second time he had taken him by surprise, Joe thought with satisfaction. He noticed Mario's set expression as the two men took their leave of him and Ellen. He could almost feel the wheels in Mario's head turning as he assessed the damage done tonight and worked on figuring an alternative plan. The one thing Joe couldn't sense in Mario was defeat. So far, he had managed to block his cousin through sheer luck. It didn't do to think how much longer his luck would last.

Once Mario and Uncle Thomas were gone, Ellen flopped back into the padded seat and sighed loudly in obvious relief.

"I was terrified he would recognize my voice after talking with me on the phone," she said. "Remind me to leave you to be hoisted on your own petard next time, Joe."

He leaned his elbow on the table and said, "You were terrific. Scotty couldn't have done any better, Ell."

"Scotty," she pronounced, grimacing, "should have had his head examined for being the rescuer. If there were a next time, I would definitely be the impulsive one."

Joe knew she was reminding him of their agreement. He let it go—for the moment. "Uncle Thomas likes you."

She smiled. "And I like him. Very much. Dammit, Joe, he would be devastated if he knew what Mario was up to. And now that I've met Mario, I . . . well, I don't feel guilty at all about helping you. If I may say so, like Cassius in Shakespeare's *Julius Caesar*, he 'has a lean and hungry look.' "

"I've always thought that," Joe said.

She nodded. "You better tell Thomas right away about Mario."

"I have no choice, really, even though he's going to be hurt. But I think Uncle Thomas will be safe enough from giving away company secrets tonight." He chuckled. "Let him enjoy Sinatra. Mario must have paid a fortune for those tickets, and it would be a shame to waste them."

"A shame," Ellen agreed, grinning.

The momentary silence between them was easy. Joe reached up and touched her hair, feeling the silkiness wrap around his fingers. Beautiful, he thought. The tendrils slid away as Ellen shifted farther around the horseshoe booth. Her movements were natural and unhurried.

"I must say I'm glad I could help you somewhat," she said in an easy tone. Her blue-green eyes were wide with apprehension, however. "Even though Uncle Thomas wasn't the man at the rink. Still, you've put your cousin on notice, I'm sure. When he realizes how futile it really is, he'll probably abandon within a day or two his crazy idea of selling the recipe."

Joe smiled at her, deciding he'd had enough of subtlety. "I like the way you so casually and adeptly put space between us like that. Any other man would think you hadn't been aware he was touching you, and you had moved over only to face him more directly."

She raised her eyebrows. "But you're going to tell me you aren't any other man, right?"

"You aren't any other woman, Ell," he replied. "I know it. And you know it."

She gazed at him steadily for one long moment,

then blinked and said, "I agreed to help you this one time, Joe. I felt I owed you that. And it was just a kiss, remember? You said so yourself. And I couldn't agree more."

He stared at her, trying to suppress his anger at her refusal to acknowledge the attraction growing between them. She *would* have to remember his stupid words too. But she had been through so much, and he sensed that the more he attempted to force her out of her shell, the more she would withdraw. He had no choice but to concede. For now.

"All right," he said, and uttered the words that seemed like a death knell. "We'll keep it light. Your mission is accomplished, Scotty, and I thank you very much for your invaluable help, without which I might possibly have managed on my own, but we will never be sure now—"

She giggled reluctantly. "You sound just like Robert Culp."

"Then let's beat it home before somebody expects me to play tennis. I'm about as good at tennis as I am at roller skating." He slid out of the booth and helped Ellen around and up on her feet. He refused to show any reaction to her touch, knowing he had to keep things light. "Thanks, really, Ellen. You were wonderful."

She smiled shyly and began walking to the lounge entrance. They had taken no more than three steps when a waitress stopped them.

"Sir, I'm sorry," she said, pushing something into his hand. "But you forgot this."

Joe looked down at the piece of paper he was holding. "Dammit! Mario stuck me with the check."

Ellen burst out laughing.

Grumbling, Joe paid the bill, leaving a generous tip. Ellen was still laughing long after the waitress disappeared and they were again on their way out of the lounge.

Although his every instinct protested the thought, Joe knew he had to let her go peacefully tonight. Ellen was vulnerable, and he had no wish to trade on that in any way. He'd have to have a plan, he decided.

One hell of a plan.

"What is Joe Carlini to you?" Lettice Kitteridge asked, the fire of determination in her eyes. "That's all I asked three days ago when you left so abruptly for Atlantic City with him and that's all I want to know now. But you, missy, have given me a load of baloney. And don't tell me this is the end of the discussion this time! I love you, and I'm concerned, and I want to know."

Ellen glared at her grandmother from across the breakfast table. Inquiring minds, she thought, were a pain in the tush. Her ravenous appetite of a moment ago for the sausage and eggs on her plate had vanished.

"And I've been telling you for three days that he asked me to go to Atlantic City, and I decided to go," she practically growled between clenched teeth. She was suddenly tired of suppressing her frustration on the subject of Joe. "That's all there is to tell. Honestly! He hasn't called again, has he? Or written, or used a carrier pigeon or satellite, or any other means of communication?"

"Did he dump you?" Lettice asked.

Ellen nearly screamed, aggravated beyond endurance. "No, he didn't dump me! There's nothing to dump from one trip to Atlantic City. For goodness' sakes, you were just yelling at me to get out more, and when I do, you complain!"

What else, she wondered, could she tell her grandmother anyway? That she went on an exciting spy hunt with a sexy man, who drew her to him as helplessly as iron to a magnet, was told she was terrific and wonderful . . . and then was dropped on the doorstep at one in the morning without a word since? She knew she shouldn't even be thinking these things herself. Her perverse mind and body needed no reminders at all where Joe Carlini was concerned.

"Well, you're moping around worse than before," Lettice snapped. "So don't tell me a tale about a casual date, young lady. Every time that phone rings, you jump and rush to answer it first."

Ellen reminded herself that she needed to explain nothing. There was nothing to explain. One time they had both agreed. And one time it had been. Whatever was happening now with Mario wasn't her business.

If it wasn't Joe himself wreaking havoc with her peace, then it was Joe's problems. She wondered for the hundredth time what was happening with Mario and the sauce. Had Uncle Thomas been saved from betrayal and embarrassment? She hoped so. He was such a sweet man. But what about the others Joe had mentioned? Had Mario gone after them too? And if he hadn't, what was he trying now? The questions had been racing around in her head for days. She had even looked up the phone number for Carlini Foods and was irritated with herself for doing so.

Damn the man, she thought, unconsciously clenching her fists. He had disrupted her peace and quiet with a vengeance. He had made her forget things she never should be forgetting. Because of him, she had been having fun when she had really only wanted . . .

"Well?" Lettice prompted.

Ellen jumped up from the table. She couldn't stand the questions from her grandmother combined with the questions in her own head any longer.

"Okay, okay. I'll confess," she exclaimed. "I was involved with Joe to stop a dastardly plot to steal a secret formula from his company. That's the only reason I went to Atlantic City with him! Now that's the real truth, Grandmother. I promise not to mope around the house and rush to answer the phone. Are you happy?"

Lettice arched her eyebrows in clear disbelief. "I suppose you'll try to sell me Grant's tomb next."

"It would be a whole lot easier," Ellen muttered, turning away from the table and the continuing argument.

Her grandmother called after her. Ellen ignored her. Blindly, she walked into the library . . . and immediately walked back out. She swerved toward the stairs, intending to go up to her room. Then she went toward the dining room again. She realized what she was doing, and stopped in the middle of the hall.

It was over with Joe, she told herself. Done.

Finished. She had been whatever help she had been, and that was that. So what if he hadn't tried to kiss her when he brought her home? Why would she want him to? She didn't, of course. She couldn't. And she had told him so. She knew she wasn't ready yet for a relationship, and she doubted if she ever would be—certainly not with someone as exciting and gentle and determined and sexy as Joe Carlini.

And if she was a little curious about what might be happening with the sauce, well, that was only human nature. Her peace and quiet had been . . . stirred up a little, that was all. Everything was now back to normal, just as she needed it, and she ought to be grateful to Joe for accepting that.

The telephone rang.

Ellen jumped for it without thinking. Before the first ring had even stopped, she yanked the receiver out of its cradle and brought it to her ear.

"Hello?" she said breathlessly, her heart beating frantically with anticipation.

"Lettice?"

Ellen swallowed back a huge wave of disappointment. "One moment please."

She put her hand over the mouthpiece and turned to call her grandmother to the telephone. Lettice was already there, eyebrows raised. Clearly, she had seen her granddaughter's mad leap for the instrument.

"For you," Ellen said sheepishly, handing over the receiver.

"A spy mission, my Aunt Muffy," Lettice said in a quelling voice. She raised the receiver to her ear. "Hello? Yes, Margery, that was Ellen playing telephone operator. . . . Yes, I'm thrilled my grand-daughter, Anne, got the Olympic equestrian team for us this year. It will be wonderful. Lovely child Anne . . ."

Ellen gritted her teeth at her grandmother's effusive tone. She walked to the front door and went outside, leaving Lettice in her grand planning stages for the annual horse show in Devon. It was a charity benefit for the children's hospital, and Ellen knew she'd be expected to put in an appearance. Life was definitely back to normal.

And she was hating every minute of it.

"Damn, damn, damn!" she muttered.

She had to rid herself of this . . . curiosity about the sauce. And she definitely had to get rid of her attraction to Joe.

She would take a drive, she decided, turning toward the garages. A long drive. And she wouldn't come back until she was rid of all thoughts of Joe Carlini.

Three hours later, Ellen strode into the kitchen. Mamie, her grandmother's housekeeper, glanced up from her dinner preparations.

"I need to use the kitchen line," Ellen announced. "And you didn't hear this conversation, okay?"

Mamie grinned at her. "Ya, sure, Ellen."

Ellen took a deep breath, told the little protesting voice inside her to shut up, then picked up the telephone and dialed.

"Carlini Foods."

She took another deep breath.

"Joe Carlini, please."

Five

"Joe Carlini, line five."

The page on the intercom echoed off the thick, impossibly white tile walls of the spice room in the Carlini Foods main processing plant.

"Dammit," Joe muttered, his concentration disrupted when he heard his name. He straightened from the small bowl on the stainless steel counter. "I think you're right, Terry. That oregano does smell . . . old. I think. It's hard for me to tell exactly what's wrong with it. I don't have the gift like you do, Terry. All I know is that the oregano is definitely not up to our standards."

"They've covered it very cleverly with some kind of oregano essence," the foreman said. "That's why I called you down here to confirm. It's subtle, but it's there."

Terry Kowalski's nose could smell a rose at a hundred paces, Joe thought gratefully. The spice room was kept immaculately clean. It had to be for those like Terry to distinguish the various scents they worked with. He frowned, hearing himself paged again. He was tempted to ignore it because of the problems here, but he knew it must be important or his secretary would have taken a message. She usually did when he was in the plant.

"Okay," he said to Terry as he walked over to the wall telephone. "I'll call Marcus Spicers. Jim Marcus won't like knowing someone's pulling this switch with his customers."

"This isn't from Marcus," Terry said. Joe turned around in surprise, and Terry added, "Mario changed spicers, Joe. I thought you knew."

Anger shot through Joe in a jolting red haze. Carlini Foods had an excellent contract with Marcus Spicers. That Mario had somehow circumvented it was appalling. And if the new spice was lousy, Joe was positive the price was higher—and that Mario was getting a kickback. That little creep wouldn't be satisfied until he'd drained the company in any way he could.

He controlled his fury enough to say, "I didn't know, Terry. I'll call Marcus and get good oregano over here right away. And I'll take care of this garbage. Anything else Mario changes, clear with me personally first."

"I'm sorry, Joe," Terry said. "He said the change was cleared in the office. I thought it wasn't right, but he's one of the family—"

"The fault is mine, not yours," Joe said. He realized that employees could be taken advantage of in a family-owned business, especially by sneaks like Mario. "I should have been more clear about his duties with everyone."

Joe turned back to the phone. He picked up the receiver and stabbed the winking button. Whoever was on the other end had better not hand him any garbage, he thought furiously.

"Hello," he snapped.

There was a tense silence, then a feminine voice said, "Joe?"

His anger drained away, and he forgot everything as he recognized the voice on the other end of the line. He knew it intimately already.

"Ellen," he said with immense relief. He had decided the best plan—temporarily—was to give her some time to cool down, and then he would call. He couldn't believe she had contacted him. She had been so adamant in Atlantic City that he would have thought pride, at the least, would have kept her from making the first move.

"Am I calling at a bad time?" she asked.

"No," he said, meaning it. His secretary had seen the picture of him giving Ellen that check at the charity dance and had even kidded him about it. She had realized he'd want to take this call. He told himself to remember to give her a raise. Smiling, he added, "It's not a bad time at all."

"Are you sure? You sound busy. Why don't I call back—"

"No," he broke in, fearing she would hang up. He remembered Terry was right behind him, so he calmed himself down before saying, "You're not disturbing me, Ell. In fact, I'm very pleased that you called."

She was silent for a moment, then said, "Well, I

was just wondering how you made out with your uncle. He was so nice to me, and I've been feeling so bad for him, knowing he'd probably be very upset when he found out about Mario."

Joe tried to suppress his disappointment. Her polite curiosity about Uncle Thomas was natural and normal. Dammit. Still, he couldn't expect anything else. She'd been so hurt in the past, she would keep herself as barricaded as possible. He ought to be glad of any kind of offering from her.

"Uncle Thomas is just fine now," he said, remembering his uncle's initial shock at his warning. And all Joe had been able to do was warn. He still had no proof of Mario's treachery. Fortunately, Thomas had already been upset that Mario hadn't taken his own mother to the show. Evidently that breach of family etiquette had offended the older man and made him wonder. Joe had said something to his cousin Jamie and sister Carol too.

"I'm glad about Uncle Thomas," Ellen said. "Well, I suppose that's that with your problem."

"I wish," Joe said.

"Oh?"

He decided it must be his imagination that he heard an eagerness behind the "oh." He continued. "A few other things have come up. I know I promised one time only, but I've been wondering if I could impose on you again. . . ."

"Well-l-l-l . . . I suppose one more time wouldn't hurt. I mean, if you really need my help. We never did find that person I saw with Mario at the rink. Is Mario meeting with him again? Is that the problem?"

"Mmmm," Joe murmured noncommittally, trying

not to lie outright. He sensed, too, that anything other than a need for her help would result in "Adios, so long, au revoir," and other forms of good-bye. "I . . . well, let's just say I have my suspicions."

"In Atlantic City again?"

"Okay." Atlantic City had its advantages, he thought. And she seemed to like it there. "Ah . . . it's tonight. Later than the last time, I think. How about if I pick you up as soon as I can get out of here, and I'll explain it all to you then, okay?"

A long silence answered him.

"Ell?"

"Okay."

When he hung up a minute later, he knew his smile had to be nearly splitting his face. He promised himself he would feel guilty later, and he turned around. Terry was staring at him in clear puzzlement.

"I'll have all of this taken care of, Terry," he said. "No problem."

Mario would survive the spice fiasco, Joe thought as he headed for his cousin's office. Just barely would Mario survive this.

Fortunately for his treacherous cousin, Joe was now in a very good mood.

Ellen had called.

She still couldn't believe she had done it.

Ellen again gazed around the Palace Casino, and out of the corner of her eye she saw Joe's smile of pure pleasure. She battled back a wave of anxiety, thinking of how quickly she'd lost her

internal struggle over him. After a long drive to
nowhere that afternoon, she had really thought
she'd brought all her frustration under control.
She had done a lot of soul-searching . . . and
remembering. And she'd been quite relaxed returning up the long driveway to her grandmother's fieldstone mansion. Until she stepped out of
the car. Before she knew it, she was in the kitchen,
dialing as if she were a madwoman. Maybe she
was. What her grandmother had had to say about
a second, even more sudden, trip to Atlantic City
was unrepeatable.

Ellen resisted the urge to giggle. Poor Lettice.

She sobered when someone jostled her against
Joe. An overwhelming urge to melt into his hard
warmth rose in her, and she fought against it,
finally straightening.

"Sorry," she muttered.

Joe dipped his head, but didn't look her way.
She didn't know whether to be relieved or hurt
that he had no reaction to her closeness. Neither
way helped her current dilemma.

The problem really wasn't that she had made
the call, she acknowledged. Any concerned person would have, especially after meeting innocent
Uncle Thomas. But one little suggestion of further help, and she had thrown herself right into it
again. If Joe had declined her new offer, she probably would have rushed down to his office and
pinned him to his desk until he'd agreed.

Suddenly her brain conjured a vivid image of
her and Joe utilizing the desktop in quite a different fashion. His hands skimming over her body . . .

"Help me, Lord," she muttered under her breath, as she desperately erased the mental picture.

"Beg pardon?" Joe asked.

"I suppose we should start looking around," she said, putting on a bright smile. What was it about Joe that made her forget everything?

Joe frowned at her. "For wha— Oh, for Mario and the man, you mean."

She nodded, wondering where his brain was. Not with hers, she hoped. Slipping gratefully into the role of spy once again, she asked, "Got any impulses, Robinson?"

He grinned at her, and she instantly felt the heat rise to her cheeks.

"For finding two men this time," she clarified, glaring at him.

"Just wander around and look," he said.

"We could always try another page."

He laughed. "You'd like that, wouldn't you? I don't think Mario would fall for it twice, do you?"

"Probably not."

"Well, we'd better look around."

As they made their way past the various gambling tables, Ellen tried not to notice Joe's fingers casually wrapped around her elbow. It was a simple gesture of male courtesy. And it also was igniting her attraction to Joe to a new high, for his hand brushed the side of her breast once, twice, three times through her silk blouse. Her breasts ached, and her mind traitorously dredged up more images of his strong fingers igniting more than attraction within her. Her heart reveled in the knowledge that they were alone. . . .

Ellen gritted her teeth and forced herself to put

more space between them. She was in big trouble if she thought that wandering through a mobbed casino was "alone." She must be nuts. Where, she wondered frantically, was her common sense? Probably out to lunch with the rest of her brain. She had to get a grip on herself. She knew more than most the unexpected ways life could hurt. She couldn't pay the price again. She wouldn't survive it.

She decided to quit torturing herself. Okay, so she'd made a little mistake. Now that she was here, she ought to forget it and just concentrate on helping Joe stop his cousin. And she should definitely stop this . . . daydreaming like a schoolgirl at a man's touch. In fact, she ought to be feeling justified about getting reinvolved with Joe and his problem, especially after what he had told her about the oregano. Mario had to be caught and stopped. Still, there must be a better way to go about it than hanging onto Joe the entire time.

"I think we should split up," she said briskly, "so we can cover more territory."

"But how would we find each other again?" Joe asked, looking at her in puzzlement. "This place is bigger than the Taj Mahal."

"Well—"

"What if you found them when I'm not with you?" he added. "By the time you found me, they could be long gone. Or if I were to see them without you, how would I know if it's the same man from the rink? You said the guy was average. Hell, that's just about everybody."

"But we might spot him sooner this time if we split up," she said lamely.

"Maybe," he conceded. "But that's about all we'd do. You're making me wonder if you're playing the impulsive spy this time."

She shrugged. "I just thought you should have a crack at being Bill Cosby."

"Very generous of you," he said, rubbing her arm and sending sensual sparks to every corner of her body. "But I like things just the way they are. Look, if we don't find them by eleven, why don't we just relax and do a little gambling in earnest? I hate losing for Mario's sake. Anyway, it's a shame to be at the shore and not even take a look at the ocean, especially at night with the moonlight glowing on the waves. . . ."

Ellen nearly moaned. He was driving her crazy.

And she had the feeling she would love every minute of it.

Eleven o'clock couldn't come soon enough, Joe thought, glancing impatiently at his watch again. Twenty more endless minutes until he could finally call a halt to this farce of searching every nook and cranny for a nonexistent meeting. Then he and Ellen could enjoy themselves.

He glanced at the woman beside him and felt guilty yet again that they were here on a wild-goose chase. When confronted with the bad oregano, Mario had made a very affecting plea, which even Joe couldn't poke a hole into, of innocently experimenting with new cost-effective sources. Joe knew that right this minute his cousin was in his office, straightening out the mess and preparing a report. Joe smiled, thinking of that report. Since

Mario was so eager to save the company money, Joe had decided a thorough investigation on the subject was in order and volunteered Mario to do the job.

As Ellen's subtle and highly sensual perfume teased his senses, Joe admitted he didn't feel *that* guilty for lying. He glanced at her, studying every curve of her body. Her tantalizing breasts, small yet perfectly shaped; the slender indentation of her waist; her long, graceful back as it flowed into her rounded hips. He didn't have to put his hands on her to know those spots intimately. His imagination had played with them from the moment she had gotten into the car.

She sighed. "Are you sure Mario was supposed to be here tonight?"

"Yes, that was what I . . . understood. Don't worry about it, Ell. It's not the end of the world if we can't find Mario this time. It's almost eleven anyway, so why don't we enjoy ourselves? I'm sure even the pros would say we were entitled."

Although her mouth pursed as if she were unsure, he could see a hint of anticipation in her eyes.

Without a word, he guided her toward the boardwalk exit. He resisted the urge to caress his fingers along the satin flesh of her arm. They'd never get out of here if he did.

"Where are we going?" she asked, taking nearly two steps to each one of his brisk strides.

"To look at some fish," he said, steering her through the gamblers.

"Fish?"

"You know. A few scales, a couple of fins, and a glassy stare."

"Okay," she said, clearly humoring him. "As long as they don't have great big jaws."

"Not a single great big jaw."

They had no sooner stepped out onto the boardwalk when Ellen pulled back. Joe turned around.

"What?" he asked.

"I don't think I want to look at some fish, Joe."

He smiled in challenge. Dammit, he'd get her to take a stroll on the boardwalk if he had to carry her.

"What's the problem with fish, Ell?"

"They smell."

He glared at her through the gloom of the erratic street lighting. "Now that you've taken any romance out of the evening, you can relax."

"As long as we understand each other."

He didn't know whether to laugh or get angry all over again when she really did relax. He finally settled for a silent chuckle. In a way, it was kind of nice to be thought of as a sex maniac ready to hustle her into the nearest bed. At least it meant she was thinking about him in physical terms.

He bowed and waved his hand with a flourish. "After you, my friend."

She eyed him for a long moment, then began to walk.

"At last," he muttered as he strode, without touching, beside her. Not touching her did nothing to stifle his awareness of her. He sensed that she, too, was aware of him.

Only a few people were strolling the boardwalk at this hour of the night, and Joe didn't plan to go far from the casino entrance. The sky was clear enough to see the stars, although the half-moon played peekaboo with several lazily drifting clouds. In the distance, the waves lapped one after the other against the wet sand. The breeze coming off the Atlantic was fresh and clean and cool.

They stopped by the railing and gazed out over the water. Ellen lifted her face, as if scenting the air like a wary doe. "I'd almost forgotten," she murmured.

"What did you forget?" Joe asked quietly, leaning his elbows on the rail.

"How soothing the ocean could be."

He smiled at the contentment in her voice. The distance between their bodies was inches, and yet they might as well have been miles apart. He shouldn't touch her, he thought. She wasn't ready. That she was actually standing alone with him was enough.

He gritted his teeth as her skirt fluttered against his legs. So close . . .

She turned around and leaned back against the railing. His internal conflict mounted at an alarming rate, for her stance thrust her breasts outward just a hand span away. He closed his eyes and decided she was torturing him. Somehow she had found out that he had brought her here under false pretenses and had set out to torture him in revenge. She was damn good at it too.

"Thank you, Joe."

He opened his eyes and turned his head. She was gazing at him, a slight smile playing around her lips.

"You're welcome," he said, his voice raspy with the need that was overtaking him.

She turned to look back at the glittering casino on the other side of the boardwalk.

She was killing him, and she didn't even know it. The hell with it, he thought, giving up the fight. One kiss. Just a taste of her was all he wanted, to confirm the kind of attraction that existed between them. He'd deal with any consequences later.

Suddenly, she gripped his arm, throwing him off balance.

"It's him!"

"What?"

She glanced at him sharply. "The man from the rink! The reason we're here. It's him!"

"But it can't be!" Joe exclaimed, his gaze sweeping the boardwalk. Nobody leaped out as distinctive to him.

"Of course it can!" she said in exasperation, pointing toward their left. "Over there. In the white windbreaker."

"But, but—"

She tugged on his arm, pulling him with her. "I'm almost positive it's the same man. I better get closer, just to be sure."

Joe had no choice but to allow himself to be dragged along with her at a near run. It couldn't be, he thought. Mario was back in Philadelphia, loaded with paperwork. He'd seen to that himself. Nobody was supposed to be here, dammit! She must have spotted someone who looked like the man at the rink. That shouldn't be hard to do, either. She had said he was "average."

When they were close enough to the man in the white windbreaker to see his face in the bright lights of the Trump Plaza Casino entrance, Ellen slowed their pace to a stroll. Joe took in the dark hair, regular features, medium build and height, and admitted the man was about as average as they come. And he had never seen him before.

"It's him," Ellen whispered fiercely, her nails digging through his suit jacket to his flesh.

"Ouch!"

"Shh. Wait."

She relaxed her hold on him, then stopped and looked up at the beautiful hotel, just as any normal tourist would. Joe helplessly followed suit. What else, he wondered, could he do? He had lied and now it was coming true. Just as he was about to kiss her, *the* man appears.

It was a punishment, he thought. A cruel and inhuman punishment. He would have gladly settled for a nose that turned into a ship's mast at the first fib. Anything was better than this.

"He's going into the Plaza," she said, interrupting his thoughts.

Joe sighed as he guided her into the casino. Who knows, he thought. He might find out who Mario's buyer was. Somehow, he didn't feel enthusiastic about the prospect.

They followed the man in the white windbreaker at a respectable distance all the way through the lobby and casino areas and into the parking garage. He was easy to tail since he strode purposefully, never stopping or deviating from the direction he was headed. Ellen's eyes sparkled with her excitement, and her skin glowed with her energy.

Joe wished he, rather than a complete stranger, had been the cause.

They lost the man, however, in the vast parking garage, since they couldn't get into the elevator with him. They could only watch the indicator for the level and go up on the next elevator. To Joe's further disgust, Ellen insisted on checking every aisle of that level. But the man was gone.

"So close," Ellen muttered, finally giving up.

So close, Joe's brain echoed, as he admitted the moment had been lost.

He vowed that Ellen was about to retire from the I Spy business.

Whether she liked it or not.

Six

Ellen had no desire to break the silence on the drive home.

As she gazed out at the dark shapes of the pine trees and the low, modern warehouses lining the north-south freeway, she almost wished she had never seen the man from the rink. Now Joe had seen him. He wouldn't need her help any longer.

It was over, and she admitted she would miss the excitement and adventure. And the fun. It had been exhilarating, a change from her drifting.

And she would miss Joe.

"I'd like to thank you, Ellen, for all your help tonight," he said, interrupting her thoughts. "You have very sharp eyes. You must be an optometrist's nightmare."

She turned to face him. His voice seemed to echo hollowly, as if he were being sarcastic, and his features looked like stone in the glow of the dashboard lights. She felt a little disappointed that he hadn't used his nickname for her. She had been growing used to it . . . even liking it.

"I was glad I could help," she said, studying the strong lines of his profile. Her blood swirled more thickly through her veins. She remembered how much she had wanted him to kiss her when they had been standing by the boardwalk's railing. It had taken every ounce of her willpower *not* to fling herself into his arms. But then she'd seen the man, and the chase was on.

Suddenly she realized that Joe wouldn't return to his own home until the very early hours, and he still had to get up and run a business in the morning. "These trips to the shore must be very hard on you, Joe."

"I'd do it again in a minute, wouldn't you?"

The sarcasm was unmistakable this time, and she sensed it was being directed at her. She couldn't understand why. All this spying business certainly hadn't been her idea.

"I'm sorry that we lost him before he connected with your cousin," she said coolly.

"That would have been the icing on tonight's cake," he agreed, then mumbled a curse.

"Dammit, Joe Carlini," she said, losing her temper. This hadn't exactly been her night either, but she wasn't sniping at him. "Save your bad mood for someone who deserves it, like your cousin Mario. *I* didn't like dropping everything to run to Atlantic City either, you know. Or taking a barrage of lectures from my grandmother, or any of the other things I've put up with to help you with your problem."

Joe gaped at her in surprise, then turned back

to the road. "I was angry with myself, Ell. I'm sorry, I hadn't realized I was taking it out on you."

She was silent for a moment as her anger dissipated. "I guess we're both tired. It's very late."

"Very."

"It probably would have made more sense to stay over in Atlantic City, than to drive home so far, so late like this," she said, speaking as the thought entered her head. "But you must need to be in the office very early."

His head swung around. "Do you mean to tell me that you would have stayed overnight with me—"

"Separately!" she exclaimed, realizing that common sense had unforeseen complications. "Separate rooms, Joe!"

He laughed. "Relax, Ellen."

"I think driving home was a better idea after all," she said in a rush.

"And let's leave it at that." He was silent for a moment. "I've been thinking . . . how would you like to see what all the fuss is about?"

She frowned. "You mean the sauce?"

"Sort of." He smiled. "I thought you might like a tour of Carlini Foods. Tomorrow, maybe? You might enjoy it."

"That's very nice, Joe," she began. "But I don't think it would be a wise idea."

"Ellen," he said patiently. "Humor me, will you? I've had a very rough day."

She knew she shouldn't. But it was so tempting to spend just a little more time with him. She liked him very much. He was . . . comfortable to be around. And yet he created feelings in her that bordered on obsession.

That was what scared her, she acknowledged. She was being pulled toward him faster and her feelings ran deeper than anything she'd ever experienced before. She was afraid to open herself again. The control she had so far exerted was a joke.

"Say yes, Ell."

She sighed. "Oh, what the hell. All right."

"Your enthusiasm overwhelms me," he said dryly.

"I'm humoring you," she reminded him. "I don't have to be enthusiastic. Would you settle, though, for curious?"

He chuckled. "I'll settle."

She leaned back in the seat and smiled to herself. Okay, so she was tempting the fates again. Just a little bit, at any rate. Besides, she really was curious to see his company. She'd been making a substantial contribution to its welfare lately.

But her relaxed state lasted only as long as it took to reach the long drive to her grandmother's Gladwyne home. Ellen's stomach tensed as Joe turned the car into the lane. Outside it was pitch black, the trees effectively blocking any source of light. Inside the car was like a warm cocoon, isolated and protected. In all the times she had been with Joe, she had never felt this alone with him before. Her heart beat faster, and her limbs felt strangely heavy. She unconsciously licked her lips, feeling their softness. She remembered the kiss outside the Four Seasons Hotel after the charity dance. Had her lips felt this soft for Joe?

Her thoughts were getting too dangerous, and

she rolled down her window a few inches to let in some much needed air. But her brain, no matter how sensible on the subject of noninvolvement, was sounding like a nag. Common sense and need just didn't mix, and right now the need was rushing through her. She knew the only thing saving her from a terrible mistake was that she was living with her grandmother. She didn't know whether to be grateful or to curse the lack of privacy.

"Well, here we are," Joe said, pulling up in front of the white-columned front portico. He shut out the headlights and turned off the Mercedes's powerful engine.

"Yes. Home at last." Ellen swallowed, aware of the small space separating them. She didn't want to look at him. She was afraid of what would happen if she did.

"Ell."

The name was like a caress. She turned, and she was lost.

Joe's face was in shadow, but it didn't matter. She didn't have to see it to know the features that had haunted her for days. Her senses caught the mingling scent of cologne and male. Her skin could feel the heat emanating from him. She was being drawn toward him at a speed that defied light.

She had to feel his mouth on hers, had to feel his tongue mating with hers, giving her life while leaving her without breath.

"Ell," he whispered, touching her cheek with one hand.

She nearly whimpered at the fingers tracing her skin. She hadn't realized how much she had been wanting this. She wanted more.

"Stop me."

She said nothing. Did nothing.

His hands reached out and gripped her upper arms, sending shock waves through her. He pulled her closer. . . .

The bright portico light came on the moment Joe's lips touched hers. They broke apart as if burned. Gasping, Ellen whipped around to see someone silhouetted in the open front door. It was easy to guess who that someone was.

"Ellen! Are you coming in?" Lettice called out. Her voice carried easily through Ellen's partially open window.

"I'm not going to the moon," Ellen muttered. She rolled the window all the way down and said, "I'll be in shortly, Grandmother. You shouldn't have waited up."

Instead of returning to the house, her grandmother walked across the porch to the passenger side of the car. She tightened the sash of her satin robe and smiled archly. "I didn't mind at all, child. Good evening, Mr. Carlini."

"Good evening, Mrs. Kitteridge," Joe said. "And please call me Joe. I'm sorry if we worried you."

Lettice nodded. "Well, it was getting very late, Joseph."

Ellen decided to kill her normally beloved relative. Lettice's sense of timing was perfect. "Thank you, Grandmother, for being concerned, but everything is just fine."

She rolled up her window in dismissal. Lettice stood next to the passenger car door, clearly refusing to take the hint.

Ellen gritted her teeth and turned back to Joe. "I have to go."

"The Dragon Lady," he said, sighing. "I don't think she likes me."

"Grandmother doesn't like anyone."

Joe grinned. "She's the perfect ending to a perfect evening."

Ellen frowned. "What are you—"

He put his forefinger against her lips. She resisted the impulse to kiss his finger.

"Never mind," he said. "Anyway, she's right. It is late. Why don't you come to the plant day after tomorrow, instead of tomorrow? That will give you a day to recover from tonight's manhunt."

She nodded. It also gave her a day to come up with a good excuse to cancel it. She still had her doubts.

"Good," he said. "There's a dire punishment if you change your mind."

She stifled a laugh at his mind reading. "Like what?"

He looked behind her and grinned. "I kiss you very thoroughly in front of your grandmother."

Her skin heated at the thought, but she wasn't sure whether it was from embarrassment or anticipation. She stared at his mouth and whispered, "I'll keep it in mind."

"Get out of the car now, Ellen Kitteridge, before I forget it's supposed to be a punishment."

"Good night, Joe," she said, opening the car door and stepping out into the night.

" 'Night, Ell."

She smiled at him and shut the door. Without a word to her grandmother, she walked into the house.

"I was concerned," Lettice began as she caught up with her.

Ellen could hear the engine of the Mercedes start up, then the hum of the tires on the pavement as the car rolled down the drive. Taking a deep breath, she said, "I love you for caring about me so much, Grandmother. And if you ever pull a stunt like that again, I will cart your prize collection of Limoges up to the roof and fling it off a piece at a time."

Lettice gasped. "You wouldn't!"

"Let's not find out, okay?" Ellen suggested and, without another word, walked up the long mahogany staircase to her bedroom.

Once inside, she pulled a videotape from her collection and pushed it into the VCR. She settled in to watch *Bull Durham*.

From his office window four stories up, Joe watched Ellen's little Audi pull into a parking space below. He breathed a sigh of relief. Even though he had called her yesterday and extracted a second promise from her to take the tour, he wouldn't have been surprised if she hadn't shown up. Sometimes dealing with her was like dealing with the mist. He never quite knew where he was. But she had come, and he considered that a major victory. The first of many, he told himself.

He picked up the two hard hats on his credenza and went down to meet her at the front doors of the executive offices. When he reached the reception area, she was already there, looking over the photographs hanging on the side wall. He nodded to the receptionist, then walked over to Ellen. She looked beautiful in a green, collarless jacket and khaki shirt and trousers. He wanted to touch her, but knew he couldn't follow through on that. His control was always precarious around her, so he was immensely grateful his hands were full at the moment. When he finally got his impulses in rein, he noticed her hair was pulled back in a tight chignon and she was wearing pumps with sensible heels.

He grinned and held out his little present for her. "Hi. Here's the latest in Paris fashions."

Ellen took the pristine white hard hat from him and held it up, admiring the intertwining C and F logo stenciled on the front. Her name was stenciled on the back.

"I love it," she said, chuckling. "I'll be the envy of all the girls on my block."

"So glad I could please," he said.

She grinned. "I had no idea, Joe, that Carlini Foods was this big. There must be ten acres of buildings."

He nodded. "Close. You've a good eye. And all of it is right down the road from the regional office of the Internal Revenue Service. It keeps the accounting department on the straight and narrow."

She giggled. "I thought I was at Fort Knox with all those guards and that barbed-wire fence surrounding the place."

"If I had known you were going to be impressed, Ell, I would have given you the two-cent tour before this. Are you ready?"

She nodded and put on the hat. It immediately sank below her eyes.

"Can you get your money back?" she asked, from under the hat.

"Naaa, it was a closeout sale," he said, tucking his own hat under his arm. He lifted hers off her head and adjusted the headband straps inside. "Here. Try it now."

She put the hat back on. It fit perfectly. "This is wonderful. One size fits all egos and frustrates the pigeons at the same time."

"You're in a good mood today," he said, guiding her through the big double doors leading to the production offices. His hand at her waist was a serious attack on his senses. "Dare I think I'm the cause?"

She laughed, but didn't answer. Instead she changed the subject. "Those pictures I was looking at were very impressive. It's a marvelous idea to show the company's growth like that. Nobody would believe this big complex originally started in a home."

He nodded, stopping just on the other side of the doors. The quiet elegance of the reception area was replaced by the hum of voices and machines. He took two white smocks off a rack and handed one to her.

"The photos were my aunt Teresa's idea, when my father moved the company here to the Northeast in the fifties. We've expanded from one warehouse and processing plant to four, plus the executive offices. We have, my friend, production offices, loading docks, truck-scale sheds, guard shacks galore, a warehouse for raw materials, a warehouse for finished products, a credit-union building, cafeterias, rest rooms, locker rooms, quality control labs, research and development—"

"Oh, my," Ellen drawled.

"Don't interrupt me, I'm on a roll. Where was I?"

"Rolling."

"Thank you. R and D. I said that already. A spice room, canning plant, separate kitchens for the sauces, pasta, soups, vegetables, bread crumbs, frozen entrees, and the fresh gourmet line. And lest I forget, a fishery room."

Ellen frowned on cue. "A fishery room? What's that?"

"That's where they process the clams, calamari, and spine fish. I warn you now, it's a room you'll love to forget."

"Okay," she said dubiously.

"Then it's showtime," he said, putting on his hard hat.

He took her everywhere and took great pride not only in showing her the entire operation, but in having her by his side. He had carefully planned their route so that they would arrive at one particular spot last. The other night had had too many interruptions, and he was taking no chances this time.

As he escorted her around the various areas of Carlini Foods, he expected her interest to be only in the tomato sauce, yet she became excited with each aspect of the tour. She tested the tomatoes, and other raw vegetables for freshness, stared in wonder at the huge vats in the soup kitchen, tasted the bread crumbs just out of the oven, shivered in the frozen food plant to watch the processing, admired the gourmet meals with the appreciation of a connoisseur, and watched the smooth economy of the canning operation. She commented on the cleanliness of the plant and giggled at the male workers who wore hair and beard nets.

In the spice room, she sniffed the air appreciatively. "It's pungent, almost overwhelming. But it smells really good."

Joe nodded, still amazed at her enthusiasm. He never would have thought she would enjoy the tour this much. In fact, they were taking longer than he had anticipated. And they still had a way to go.

He laughed when she walked unsuspecting into the fishery room and immediately walked out again.

"Good Lord!" she exclaimed. "Now that's pungent. What's in there? Moby Dick?"

"One would think so," he agreed.

"I'll just watch from here," she said, looking through the glass portal in the double doors.

He had saved the sauce kitchen for next to last. He took her into the quality control lab room, got a little bowl out, and filled it with a couple of tablespoons of the current batch waiting to be taste tested.

He set the bowl and a flat wooden spoon onto the stainless steel counter in front of her.

"So this is it," she said, eyeing the thick red sauce. Bits of tomato, onion, and spices swirled invitingly throughout.

"This is it."

"Worth millions."

"Priceless, actually."

"Hard to believe."

"Believe it."

Joe grinned as Ellen picked up the spoon and carefully tasted the sauce.

She straightened and, with a mischievous glint in her eye, said, "Not bad."

"Not bad!" came a voice from behind her. "That's great sauce, lady. Good solid flavor, fine texture, pleasing bouquet. The best batch we've ever made!"

She turned around to find a young man grinning at them.

Joe grinned back. Miguel Sanchez was the assistant foreman of the process vats, and he was continually fighting with the quality control people over the taste and feel of the sauces. " 'Morning, Miguel. And all the sauce batches are the best ever according to you. You just want to get out of here by five."

Miguel laughed. "Hey, Mr. Carlini. Is this the new health inspector? If it is, I think I'm gonna enjoy inspections from now on."

"This," Joe said in a warning tone, "is Ellen Kitteridge. And she is not the health inspector."

"It figures," Miguel said. "No breaks for the working man."

"Ell, meet Miguel Sanchez, who's just leaving," Joe said, hinting blatantly.

Ellen smiled at him and held out her hand. "It's nice to meet you, Mr. Sanchez."

With a flourish the assistant foreman lifted her hand to his lips and kissed it. "A real pleasure, beautiful lady."

"Miguel thinks he's the reincarnation of Don Juan," Joe said, glaring at his employee. Miguel was a little too charming to suit him. "He's going to be the reincarnation of an unemployed man if he doesn't get back to work."

"Good-bye, lovely lady," Miguel said, without

blinking an eye. "I've got to go talk to my union rep about the lousy working conditions in this joint."

The young man strolled away. Ellen laughed. "He's a character."

"He's a something all right, but I like him anyway," Joe said. Okay, so he was jealous, he thought. He was entitled. He turned to her. "To pick up where we were so rudely interrupted: What do you mean the sauce is 'not bad'?"

She smiled. "I mean the sauce is not bad, which is better than the sauce is not good."

"It's great sauce!" Joe said, and proceeded to quote his assistant foreman. "Good solid flavor, fine texture, pleasing bouquet. The best batch we've ever made!"

She laughed and licked the spoon again.

Joe took the utensil out of her hand. "For 'not bad' sauce you seem to like it. You've licked the spoon clean."

"Caught, darn it," she said, shaking her head. Then she grew serious. "It's excellent, really."

"You sound surprised."

"I am a little," she admitted. "Does that make me a food snob?"

"Probably, but don't lose sleep over it," he said, taking her arm.

She visibly stiffened, as if jolted by lightning. Joe knew she had been. The shock of his own response to their touching was rocketing through him too. With her, it came out of nowhere, he thought. Unexpected and overwhelming. He was more than ready for their last stop.

"Do you cook?" he asked, his voice hoarse. They

had to talk about something, otherwise he wouldn't be responsible for his actions.

She didn't look at him, but she didn't pull away either. Finally she said, "I used to. Where are we going?"

"The last stop," he said, and led her toward their final destination on the tour.

When they reached yet another set of wide double doors, he pushed them open, and they walked into a huge warehouse the size of two airplane hangars. As far as the eye could see were cardboard cases of bottled spaghetti sauce stacked in pallets six high. Forklifts whizzed in and out the open bay doors to their left. Nobody seemed to notice them at all.

"The Carlini fortune," Joe said with pride.

"Is all this sauce?" Ellen asked, staring in wonder at the sight before her.

"In one form or another. This way."

He escorted her down the main aisle between the pallets until they were far from the noise and the workers. He turned right through a narrow passage between the tall stacks. Cases towered above her head. He turned right again down another passage and stopped. He spun her around, bringing her so close they were touching breast to chest, hip to hip, and thigh to thigh in the narrow space.

"What's back here?" Ellen asked. Her voice was breathless. She tried to edge away from him, but there was nowhere to edge to.

Joe gazed down at her. The lunch whistle blew. Right on cue, he thought dimly, his mind and body succumbing to her presence. Her eyes were wide with anticipation and tension. The slim column of her neck was arched invitingly toward him. Her skin was impossibly silken, and her lips were flawlessly made. Why had he ever thought she wasn't perfect? She was.

He had lived through two days of torture for this moment. The tour had been a joy and an agony. He had planned their route to the finest detail, insuring that they would end up here, in the vast, darkened warehouse. Now he allowed himself to feel what he had been holding back since she first drove onto the premises. This time nothing was going to interrupt them.

"You and I are alone back here, Ell," he said.

"Joe, I don't know—"

"I don't know either," he said, cupping her face in his hands. He pressed her back against the cases until her soft curves were crushed against his hard muscles. "But we're going to find out. Now."

He lowered his mouth to hers.

Seven

Even as she clung to him, Ellen told herself she shouldn't have come on the tour. She had known something like this would happen.

Still, she couldn't stop herself from responding to his kiss. She needed this, needed Joe's mouth on hers and his arms around her, needed his hands skimming across her back. His body was pressed against hers, and she could feel every inch of flesh and bone and muscle. Their clothes were a thin barrier between them.

His tongue mated knowingly with hers, teasing her senses. She could feel her desire gladly meeting his. His hands kneaded her derriere and lifted her into him. She wanted to cry out in satisfaction and need. The kiss was like a lifeline, forcing her to reach out and accept it. Accept Joe.

A thread of panic spun through her, and she tore her mouth away from his.

"I'm not ready," she whispered, gasping for breath. "I'm not ready."

"Yes, you are," he whispered back, crowding her against the cases.

"No." Even as she said it, her hips pressed to his in denial of the word.

His hands slid between them to capture her breasts. Ellen moaned as his fingers worked her nipples through the barrier of clothing. She took a deep, shuddering breath, trying to force back the heavy drowning waves coursing through her veins. The man certainly knew how to give a tour, she thought.

"Joe, please," she said in lame protest.

"Please what, Ell?" he asked, his hips nudging softly at hers.

"Please don't stop."

His lips instantly found hers, and she was lost in mindless pleasure. It was voices, two men laughing loudly on the other side of the cases, that finally made them break apart a few moments later.

Ellen felt as if she had been through a whirlwind. She could feel her hair, so tight in its bun before, now loose and flopping on her neck. It was horrifying to think what the rest of her might look like. She had no idea what would have happened if people hadn't wandered by, but if she could hear them, then it was possible they could hear . . .

She straightened and side-stepped away from Joe. His eyes were glazed, and his cheekbones were tinged with passion. She knew she had done that to him, and she didn't know whether to be pleased or ashamed.

She had to make light of this, she thought. Mature adults kissed all the time, so it was silly to make a fuss about it.

Clearing her throat, she said, "I had no idea a warehouse was so . . . interesting."

"I saved the best part for last," he said, tucking in his shirt.

She forced herself to reach up and straighten his tie, as if it were a commonplace action. "There's lipstick on your cheek. Give me your handkerchief."

He pulled a pristine white one from his pocket and handed it to her.

"Do you always bring women into the warehouse and kiss the life out of them?" she asked in as casual a tone as she could muster, while wiping at the imprint.

"Only on the third Tuesday of the month," he replied. He touched her cheek. "Ell?"

Her attempt at lightness collapsed at the tender gesture.

"I don't know," she said brokenly. "I lost too much the last time. I don't think I can go through it again, and nobody can guarantee me that I won't. Can you?"

He was silent for a long moment, then said, "No, I can't. So we'll go slow. How about lunch to start?"

She wasn't sure she wanted to go anywhere, but she managed a laugh at the abrupt change of subject. "That's slow?"

He grinned. "Sure. We've got a dining room in the executive offices. It's part of the tour."

Ellen admitted to herself that she didn't know what she wanted. But the more she was with Joe,

the more she wanted him. She was at a cross-
roads, and she knew it. Still, she thought, a free
lunch wasn't a bad deal.

She nodded, straightening her hair as best she
could without a mirror. "All Carlini Food products, I'll bet."

He leaned forward. "Don't tell anyone, but we've
been known to sneak in a Pat's cheesesteak upon
occasion. Ready?"

She giggled. "Ready."

He escorted her with great dignity out into the
open, and this time the warehouse was nearly
deserted. Once more nobody, to her relief, looked
particularly interested in them. Maybe everyone
did think she was the new health inspector. She
hoped so.

They walked through the executive offices and
into the dining room. The green-striped wallpaper
and Queen Anne-style furniture made for elegant
surroundings. A visitor would be impressed with
the company's obviously thriving prosperity.

The room was crowded with people eating lunch.
Realizing a good portion of them must be Joe's
relatives, she batted down a huge wave of butter-
flies. She had momentarily forgotten this was a
family business. Then she spotted Mario. He was
staring at her, his eyes narrowed and calculating.
A shiver ran down her spine, and she had a strong
notion she was being dissected for possible use.

Joe touched her elbow. "This way. I've got a
table reserved."

Before they could move, Uncle Thomas was waving and hurrying toward them.

"Joey, you brought Ellen!" the older man exclaimed, when he reached them. He kissed her on the cheek as if he had known her for years.

"It's nice to see you again," Ellen said, smiling at him. It *was* nice.

"Quit flirting, Uncle Thomas," Joe said, tightening his grip on her elbow. "Otherwise I'll be forced to be jealous."

Thomas smiled happily. "As if I stood a chance, Joey. Come, Ellen, let me introduce you to some of the family."

Ellen innocently walked into the lion's den with a lamb, in the form of Uncle Thomas, leading the way. She had no idea just how far she had entrapped herself until the older man stopped at the first table.

"This is Ellen Kitteridge, Joey's girl," Thomas announced proudly to the two women at the table.

Ellen froze.

"Joey's girl?" the women echoed in unison, their expressions lit up with eager speculation.

"This is Joe's aunt Teresa and cousin Marlene, Ellen."

Ellen wished the floor would open up and swallow her whole. Unfortunately, the damn thing refused to cooperate, and she was left to shake hands with Teresa and Marlene. "I'm just a friend," she said.

"I should be so lucky," Thomas said, winking broadly.

"Ahh . . . Uncle Thomas," Joe began.

But Uncle Thomas was unstoppable as he launched into the story of meeting the two of them in Atlantic City. Clearly, Ellen thought, when Joe had explained to Thomas what Mario was up to, he had neglected to correct any notions of her being a "date" that evening.

She glared at Joe. He shrugged. She was tempted to find the nearest samurai sword and put it to good use. She wondered in mortification how she could have believed Uncle Thomas was a sweet, kindly man. To her further irritation, she became aware of Joe smothering amusement when Teresa asked him if he was bringing Ellen to a christening on Sunday.

"Oh, I don't think so," she said, at the same time Joe said, "Of course. It's for my nephew," he added to Ellen. "I was going to ask you, but the family just beat me to it."

She smiled sweetly at him. "We'll discuss it later."

But the damage was done. Thomas's voice had carried to the next tables, and suddenly people were calling out for introductions to "Joey's girl." Everyone ignored her corrections, and they all insisted Joe bring her to Sunday's christening to meet the rest of the family. Sensitive to all the speculative glances, Ellen suspected Joe's family was more interested in her "celebrity" status than in her being Joe's new girlfriend.

Joe was smiling and accepting the attention, as if there were nothing extraordinary about it. What, she wondered, could she expect, after the way she had just kissed him?

She was torn between being angry with him and with herself for this mix-up. And she had no idea how to correct it.

Wonderful, she thought. It looked as if she were going to a Carlini christening.

As Joey's girl.

•   •   •

"I can't."

Joe held his temper at the words. It was after lunch, and he and Ellen were standing in the lobby. He could feel the company receptionist craning to hear their conversation. Keeping his tone low and even, he said, "I know my family got carried away, Ell, but—"

She shook her head. "Going to the . . . communion—"

"Christening. For my nephew. My sister Carol's baby."

"Yes. I'll do that. I said I would."

"And I said I was sorry about Uncle Thomas's misunderstanding."

She narrowed her eyes for an instant, her body tensing. Watching her, he figured his family must have grated even more than he had thought.

Finally she sighed and relaxed again. "I know. But you should have told him the truth about me, Joe. Then this wouldn't have happened."

He ran his fingers through his hair in frustration at the twin urges to shake her and kiss her. Both sounded satisfying. "I told him you were helping me with Mario. I thought he understood. How was I to know he had jumped to conclusions and assumed we were involved with each other and that's *why* you were helping me."

She waved a hand. "I guess it couldn't be helped. Joe, I do understand that you have to keep up this farce for a little while longer—"

"It's not a farce, Ell. Just a dinner invitation." Joe scrambled for something to get her to agree. Maybe she only needed a little push. After all, her protest sounded halfhearted. "I merely asked you to have dinner with me tonight. What's wrong with that? Mario's 'contained' for the moment, so why don't we relax and get to know each other better?" Her body tensed again, and he knew he'd made a mistake. Backtracking, he added, "I'd like to do something to show my appreciation for all your help."

"Then send me flowers."

"I'll pick you up at eight," he snapped, his exasperation getting the best of him. Why couldn't just one thing be easy with her? Because she'd been hurt as very few people had, he answered himself.

"Joe—"

"Eight o'clock."

"No. I'm not ready."

He stared into her wide eyes. Why wouldn't she acknowledge what was between them? He corrected himself. She acknowledged it. The problem was she was afraid to do something about it.

"You'd better hurry," he said, grinning. "You've got a little more than four hours to get ready. I'd walk you to your car, but that would give you time to think up an excuse. And I'm not accepting excuses today. Remember that."

He walked away through the double doors before she could protest his Neanderthal tactics. He should have known a simple invitation to dinner wouldn't be so simple with Ellen. Nothing worth having ever was.

"But she's not here, Joseph."

Joe gaped at Ellen's grandmother as she stood

in the doorway of her Gladwyne home. He was dimly aware of a slow flush of anger rising up his neck to his face. He hadn't once considered that Ellen might stand him up.

"I'll wring her neck," he finally said.

"I assume from that remark that she was supposed to be here," Lettice said, eyeing him.

"I told her I would pick her up at eight for dinner," he replied, numb with the shock of her defection. He should have realized she would panic. He'd pushed too hard. Suddenly he was angry with himself. "How could I be so stupid?"

"One does wonder." Lettice took the bouquet of flowers from his stiff fingers. "We might as well get these in water before you crush the freesias and daisies any further. You better come in, Joseph. You look as though you could use a drink."

The offer was surprising coming from the dragon lady, but he didn't have time for it. "Where is she?"

"Not until you're calm. Now come inside."

The imperious tone penetrated the red haze that was building inside him. He opened his mouth to say he was calm, but Lettice had already turned on her heel and was walking back into the house. He had no choice but to follow her—if he wanted to know where Ellen was.

Lettice took him into a little solarium off the kitchen. It was filled with plants of all kinds, and Joe stared at the vibrantly colored orchids in bloom along one wall. She stopped at a work counter and began to fuss with the bouquet.

"There's a bottle of whiskey and some glasses in

that cabinet there," she said, dipping her head to her left.

"No thanks."

"Then make one for me. A little water and no ice. Ice ruins a good grain." She smiled slightly. "I learned that in Scotland."

Joe swallowed back his impatience and made the drink. He handed it over.

Lettice took a healthy sip, then said, "Actually, I don't know where she is."

He glared at the older woman. "Then why didn't you tell me that before—"

"Because you've turned her upside down, young man," she said, arching an eyebrow. "She ran out of here as if it were the great escape. Any fool can figure out there's something between you two. I want to know exactly what it is."

Joe felt as if someone had just punched him in the solar plexus.

Lettice chuckled. "Took the wind out of your sails, didn't I?"

"Yes," he admitted.

"Then I'll take them out some more. What are your intentions concerning my granddaughter?"

"I . . ." He paused. "To be honest, I don't know. I only know she turns *me* upside down. I'm willing to go wherever it leads. And in case this is the reason for the third degree: I don't give a damn that her family came over on the Mayflower or that she has enough trust funds to bankroll an entire country. I've got my own money and my own name, and I like them just fine."

Lettice gazed at him. He gazed back.

"I'll accept that," she said at last. "And if you

hurt her, I'll come after you with everything I've got. She's been hurt too much."

"I know," he said. He was beginning to like Ellen's grandmother.

Lettice nodded. "Now that we understand each other . . . I might not know where she is, but I have a good idea where you could look."

Ellen glided around the roller rink, unconsciously avoiding the other skaters as her tensions drained out of her.

It felt good to be on skates, she thought. It felt good, too, to be at the rink nearest to home. No more hiding in Jersey. Teenagers dominated the rink this evening, and two boys whooshed by her. They were so close that one misstep would have knocked her off her feet.

And she would have deserved it.

She had no sooner set foot in the rink than the guilt of skipping out on Joe had assailed her. Okay, so he had ordered her to dinner. The man had been entitled to his frustration when she had refused the date. After all, she had kissed him as if she were starving for him.

No wonder he was confused. She was confused. But it was just that dinner seemed so . . . intimate. Candlelight and champagne reminded her too much of sensuality and seduction. She wasn't ready for that. She wasn't ready for Joe Carlini to be in her life. And he was already there. Tours and christenings and dinners were too fast for her. She was fine when they were charging after his cousin Mario. But beyond that, she panicked.

She knew she was afraid to be hurt again, and it was easier to avoid anything resembling a relationship, including dinner. The kiss seared through her mind again, and she groaned.

"Just as if he were the last man on earth, and you were really glad to see him," Ellen muttered to herself in disgust.

"Problem, lady?"

Startled, she turned to discover one of the rink's referees hovering. Clearly, he'd heard her mumblings and thought she was speaking to him. She blushed and gave him a sheepish smile. "Sorry. Just grumbling to myself over the latest headlines."

The referee looked blank, then he nodded and skated past. Good thing, too, Ellen thought with a widening smile. She had no idea what the latest headlines were either.

Her amusement subsided when she noticed a young boy and girl by the locker area. The two teenagers were standing together in the flush of growing sexuality, and she slowed as she couldn't help watching them. The girl's fingers caressed a button on the boy's denim jacket. His hand tightened on her hip in response. The girl looked up at the same moment his head lowered, and he took her mouth in a deep kiss.

Ellen felt her face heat again for a different reason. She wrapped her arms around her waist and skated faster, determined to put the scene behind her. Everything was so uncomplicated to teenagers, she thought with envy.

Then someone all too familiar caught her attention. She stumbled over her roller skates as she recognized Joe standing on the other side of the curving barrier separating the rink proper from the rest of the building. She managed to save herself from a humiliating fall on her backside. He was staring at her, his expression giving away nothing.

How, she wondered frantically, had he found her? She had thought no one would find her here. In fact, she had thought no one would even bother to look. She should have known better than to think she could get away from Joe.

She realized she had to go over to him. To do anything else would only make her look more foolish than she already was.

Trying to control her nervousness, she carefully picked her way through the rambunctious young skaters. She stopped when she reached the barrier, grateful for the space between them.

"I wish you would have told me you wanted to eat here," he said in the calmest of voices.

His matter-of-fact attitude bewildered her. She had been preparing for an outburst of anger.

"I . . . ah . . . well, pizza and soda seemed just fine to me," she said helplessly, waving toward the snack bar.

He gave her a brief smile. "I have something better in mind. Let's go. I'm starving."

Feeling trapped, she came around the open end of the barrier and joined him on the other side. He didn't touch her, and for a moment she thought he was too furious with her to do so. Yet as he walked beside her, saying nothing, she realized he was disappointed, as if she had hurt him. She had never meant to do that. It had only been her own fears riding her that had made her act so . . . selfishly.

She nearly groaned aloud when they reached the locker bay. The boy and girl were still there. They had retreated to a shadowy corner and were now wrapped in each other's arms, oblivious to anything around them. Just what she needed, she thought, as she inserted the key in her locker. A full-blown demonstration of what she was refusing to acknowledge. At least the teenagers were behind her and she could turn her back on the worst of it. She refused to look at Joe, and at the same time realized how much that refusal merely heightened her awareness of him.

"How did you find me?" she asked, hoping to dispel the urge to caress his suit buttons in imitation of the girl's earlier gesture.

He glanced over at the couple, then returned his gaze to her. She could feel him take in her profile, her throat, her breasts. Her oxford cotton blouse, she knew, was more like see-through net to his gaze. Her blood throbbed in her veins.

"Common sense," he said at last. "You skate to work off your feelings. That's been obvious from the first. And now that your grandmother knows you skate, you don't have to go to Jersey anymore. I just started with the rink closest to your home and found you first time out."

"I didn't know I was so obvious," she said.

"You're not."

A moan of pleasure came from the shadows behind them, stilling all conversation. Her hands stopped the task of pulling her things from the locker. Her body temperature rose sharply, and she couldn't quite catch her breath. How could a couple of kids necking do this to her? And then she realized it wasn't the kids.

It was Joe.

The raw edge of suppressed male passion reached out to her, burrowing its way into her body, intensifying her emotions. His heat, bare inches from her, was like a blast furnace, turning her to molten liquid. She could hear the breath rasping in his lungs. The remembered taste of his mouth on hers flashed through her, vivid and enticing. She wanted to turn to him, to toy with the buttons of his jacket, to feel his hand tighten on her hip, then pull her into a deep kiss. He didn't have to touch her to get a response, and he had to know it. He could take her right here, and she doubted she'd have the power to stop him. She thought she would die of embarrassment . . . and want.

"Kids," he muttered hoarsely. "Get your stuff, Ell."

Eight

"Now dinner wasn't so bad, was it?"

Joe glanced over at Ellen and chuckled as she made a face at him. They were on their way home after an easy meal. Maybe not easy, he admitted, remembering the occasional moments of tension. Since the near eruption of passion at the skating rink, both of them had kept their attraction under tight control. Still, dinner went better than he would have thought, especially after seeing those damn kids at the rink. Hadn't they ever heard of parking?

"Delicious, actually," Ellen conceded, then waved a hand at her sweater and jeans. "But did you have to take me to the Cafe Royale dressed like this?"

"That was where I made the reservation." He watched the evening traffic with a prudent eye. Center-city Philadelphia could match New York

City for the "nuts on the road" award. He added, "Don't blame me, just because you weren't ready."

She was silent for a long moment. "Your idea of slow is the speed of light."

He smiled. "And your idea of slow would make a snail look like a racehorse."

"I panicked over the idea of dinner. I admit that. But I'm not . . . I don't know what I'm not. I'm just not."

"Eloquently put." He glanced over at her. "You make me impatient, Ell. So you'll have to be patient with me."

She smiled slightly. "If you can be patient with me."

"Agreed."

Joe hid a burst of satisfaction. At least she recognized there was something to be patient about. That ought to be enough for him. As long as he didn't touch her.

He set his jaw, thinking that he might as well stop breathing. The results would be the same. The problem was that this was their first date. It was just a dinner, he told himself in an attempt to keep the adrenaline coursing through him under some control. But it was nearly impossible, since he knew they weren't on a mission to save the sauce. Or a pretense of a mission to save the sauce. They were on a date.

"I noticed Mario in the company dining room at the plant," Ellen said, breaking into his thoughts. "I meant to ask you if he's made another attempt at the recipe."

"Not yet," he replied, looking over at her. Her features held a translucent glow that left him staring in awe. He realized what he was doing and turned back to the road. To cover his discomposure, he added, "Even though it's only been a few days, he's been too quiet, and that worries me. I think Uncle Thomas was his best shot at getting a second piece of the recipe. Thomas was the easiest. My cousin Jamie, who holds another quarter, is one of the company lawyers. He's too smart to be tricked into giving it away. I hope. Anyway, my sister at least wouldn't be fooled. But I can't help feeling Mario is only biding his time."

"You still have no proof against him?" she asked, her voice even and calm. He could see nothing in her of the turmoil he was feeling. "What about your uncle? Couldn't he support you, if you told your family about what Mario is doing?"

"How?" Joe asked, his hands tightening on the steering wheel when he thought of how thoroughly he was trapped in family politics. "All Mario really did was to treat his uncle to a night in Atlantic City. Thomas knows and understands I can't fire Mario on suspicion, because of family repercussions. It'll be bad enough when I do catch him. His mother, my aunt Mary, is going to be devastated. She dotes on him. That's a lot of the problem."

"You said he needed money," Ellen said, in a speculative tone. "Maybe she's giving him money."

He shook his head. "She and his father had a huge fight several months ago about that. His father did manage to cut off that source of money from Mario. I do know Mario's spending didn't slow at all. He's desperate now. I have a feeling the only way I'll catch him is for him to be careless."

He resisted the urge to vent his frustration.

Tonight was his first real opportunity to further the relationship with her, and here she had managed to get him thinking about his cousin. It was like thinking of baseball at the crucial moment of lovemaking. No one wanted to, but it was damn effective.

He became aware that Ellen was quiet, too, and he glanced over to find her expression far away.

"Thinking can be hazardous to one's health," he said, stopping at a red light.

She took a deep breath and refocused on the road ahead of them. "I know."

She didn't add anything to her answer and instead reached over and turned on the car radio. Hard, driving rock and roll blasted from the speakers. He grabbed for the volume dial the same moment she did.

Their fingers touched, and Joe was plunged into a well of desire for her, endless and enveloping. She snatched her hand away, but it was too late for him. His breath labored in his lungs, his body tensed, his blood pounded in his ears. The road faded for an instant, then he forced himself to control the primitive urges racing through him. The light had changed and horns were beeping behind him. He stepped on the accelerator.

Once the car was across the intersection, he turned off the radio. He could hear Ellen breathing hard. She was sitting as far away from him as the passenger seat would allow. She didn't look unaffected now. He decided he had been much better off discussing business with her. At least they had a good chance of getting home in one piece. He was president of a company that had survived going national and a takeover attempt last year. He was supposed to have ice in his veins, not the raging heat of a hormone-crazy adolescent.

"Okay, so now you know my deep, dark secret. I like hard rock," he confessed, knowing he had to keep it light if he was ever to get through the trip home. "I can't help it. I grew up in the sixties. Give me an Eric Clapton album and I'm a happy man."

Ellen relaxed. He was pleased she even managed a giggle. She turned the radio back on, but adjusted the volume to a more manageable level. "You'll be warped for life, you know."

He smiled. "I expect so."

It was after eleven when they reached the parking lot of the roller rink, where Ellen's car was still parked. Joe breathed a sigh of relief that they had made it without further mishap. The conversation between them had been as light as helium. It kept the existing tensions on an even keel.

Ellen's Audi sat in solitary majesty in the lot. Joe gritted his teeth at the sight of the empty parking spaces and dim lighting surrounding the car. He hadn't considered that the rink would be closed and the people gone. As he pulled his car next to the driver's side of the Audi, he vowed he would not touch her. Just like when they had been trapped next to those two entwined teenagers by the lockers, or when their fingers had touched, he could feel the desire to take her in his arms climbing toward a frenzied peak. He had been afraid to touch her at the rink, afraid he wouldn't be able to stop himself. Now his need had had all evening to simmer.

"It was a very nice dinner," Ellen said, her voice low.

He could sense her anxiety, and he knew he had to end this date companionably. If he wanted to see her again. And he did. He had promised her "slow," and now he had to deliver. He deliberately relaxed and turned in the seat to face her. She was facing forward, and her hand was gripping the door latch. Her clear readiness to bolt brought a sudden surge of protectiveness for her.

"It was a terrific dinner . . . once I found you," he said, keeping his tone amused. "Next time you run away, please dress for it."

She chuckled a little, shaking her head. "I probably will, just in case you catch me again."

"No probably about it." He smiled to himself, noting the tension in her fading. His own tension was slowly draining away too. No problem, he thought. He'd just remind her about the christening on Sunday, they'd say good night, she'd get out of the car, and that would be that. "Don't forget the christening on Sunday. I'll pick you up about one, okay?"

She smiled. He watched with satisfaction as her hand let go of the door latch. "That's fine."

"I'll follow you home," he said, not liking the idea of her going on alone.

"Thank you, but no." Her smile widened. "I'm Scotty, the sensible spy, remember? I can certainly drive myself home."

"Maybe I'm the one we ought to be worrying about."

"You'll do just fine."

"So far," he muttered to himself, knowing she was capable of driving herself home but having a vague feeling Miss Manners wouldn't quite approve. "One o'clock then on Sunday. And you're sure you don't need an escort?"

She nodded. "I'm sure. Good night, Joe, and thanks for dinner."

"Good night, Ell, and you're welcome." Part two of his game plan was completed. Tough as it was, he admitted he was satisfied.

She opened the passenger door, then turned around. "Oh! I'm almost forgetting my skates. They're on the back seat."

"Right, right, right. The skates," he said, and stretched around to retrieve them.

He collided instead with soft shoulders and reaching, feminine arms intent on the same purpose. He scrambled back into his seat away from her, scorched by the sudden fire exploding within him. The breath left his body, and at the same moment his senses were filled with the scents of perfume and woman. His blood pounded beyond its limits.

He stared at her, the space separating them almost nothing. Her eyes were wide and focused on his, and her full lips were parted. His earlier thoughts of her being unaffected by the attraction between them vanished. A sensual challenge filled the air. A primitive part of him dared him to respond. He told himself to ignore it, let it go, take a cold shower, move to the Arctic Circle . . . then he saw the tip of her tongue slip slowly along her lower lip, moistening it, and he was lost.

Without thought, he pulled her to him, bringing her mouth to his. Her lips were softer than he'd remembered, and they molded to his under the onslaught of his kiss. He parted her lips, his tongue delving inside to claim hers. She met him eagerly, the clash and duel of the kiss consuming him. Her arms wound around his shoulders, her fingers digging into his suit jacket.

He had never expected her to respond like this. She wasn't fighting him at all, and he had no thought to fight himself. He pressed her closer until her breasts were against his chest. He slipped his hand around and under her sweater, gliding across the flawless silk of her skin. The front hooks of her bra were undone with a press of his fingers. One breast spilled free of the satin and into his waiting hand. The nipple, already tight, leaped against his palm as if his touch were giving it life. He tore his mouth from hers and dipped his head lower, determined to taste her in a way he never had before.

Her hands were clinging and tugging as he nuzzled her breasts. The taste of her was smooth and fine, like a wine that had come into its full bouquet. Her flesh had a scent of its own, heady and intoxicating. He started with slow, light kisses everywhere he could reach, his hands charting a path before his lips, finding new curves and dips to explore. His kisses became more fierce as he drowned in the taste of her. He heard a low moan, when he finally curved his tongue around the diamond-hard nipple. The satisfaction was unlike anything he'd felt before, and yet his need was driven to the breaking point.

Ellen felt as if years of repression had slid away with the kiss. The touch, she corrected herself dimly, as Joe's mouth sent a kaleidoscope of sensations racing through her. She had lost all thought of resistance the moment their bodies had touched in the quest for the skates. She had tried her best to fight this. She had even run away from it tonight. But throughout dinner and the ride back to the rink, she had been tormented with the thought that the evening would end like this. Her in his arms, out of control. She had wanted it to happen, and when he had pulled away from her, she had willed it to happen.

She was out of control now, she realized as her fingers found their way under his suit jacket. She could feel the muscles of his back working under his fine cotton shirt whenever he moved. His hands were touching her everywhere, seeking out every pleasure spot she possessed. His mouth was the center of her being, driving her to distraction. She was moaning shamelessly under his caresses, and she didn't care. She used her hands to guide his lips over her flesh, and she thrust her breasts forward so he could taste all of her. He was taking her body and mind to places unimagined before. Something ageless inside her had been brought to life again. Now it was growing and calling out to him. It didn't matter where they were, or who they were, or what consequences she would face afterwards. She could no more stop this than she could stop breathing.

He lifted his head, and at the sudden shock of her nipple bereft of his mouth she really did stop breathing.

"We can't," he said, his voice hoarse.

She blinked, stunned by the words. He was kidding, joking with her. She could hear the need in his voice. His arms were still tight around her, and her bared breasts were against his chest, the fabric of his shirt teasing her wildly sensitive nipples.

"Joe, please," she whispered, struggling to push off his jacket.

He captured her hands and held them between their bodies. "I won't make love to you in a car, Ellen Kitteridge. Not the first time."

She blinked again, stilling her efforts to escape his grasp.

He buried his face in her neck. "And I won't make love to you too soon, Ell. Even if you've momentarily forgotten it, this is too soon."

Shaken, she closed her eyes, feeling her need swirling deep and heavy inside her. It was like being slammed against a wall of reality, she thought.

"I wish you weren't so smart," she finally said, trying to bring herself under control.

He collapsed, half on, half off her, his chest shaking with his amusement. "Either that, or you stop being so damn sexy."

She was torn between anger and relief. She opted instead for being pleased that he thought her sexy. And he had cared more for her emotional well-being than for his physical satisfaction. Most men wouldn't. He must have known she wouldn't have stopped him. He was keeping his promise to her. Something inside her broke at the thought.

The armrest was pressing uncomfortably into her back, and to cover the sudden rush of tenderness from showing, she said, "My back is killing me. However do the kids manage this?"

"In my parking days, way back around the Middle Ages, I don't remember the steering wheel getting in the way this much." He kissed her lightly on the mouth in what should have been a brotherly fashion and almost wasn't. He immediately straightened, then groaned loudly. "Either steering wheels are getting bigger, or I'm way out of shape."

"You're way out of shape."

"Thanks."

"You're welcome." She adjusted her clothes and sank back in the car seat. Her hands were shaking and heat was rushing to her cheeks. Her mind whirled with confusion. The more she tried to resist him, the more she ached to give in to him. She didn't know what to think anymore, and yet all her thoughts were filled with Joe.

His hand curved around her jaw, and he turned her toward him. His face reflected his concern. "Are you okay?"

She smiled slightly and nodded. "I'm fine."

His fingers were warm and strong against her cheek. Her breathing quickened, and desire, barely suppressed, began to swirl through her again. He leaned forward and touched her lips lightly with his. Again . . . and again.

"We'd better stop this now," he said between kisses.

"We should," she agreed, not moving.

"We could . . ." His voice trailed away as he kissed her thoroughly this time.

When they finally resurfaced, they broke apart. Ellen was better prepared this time for the deprivation. She took a deep breath and brushed the hair back from her shoulders. "I'd better go."

He reached in the back and got her skates. She held the clunky objects on her lap for a second, then opened the car door.

"Dinner, tomorrow?" he asked. "No parking, I promise."

She hesitated, then nodded. "Yes."

"Good." He started laughing. "What if a cop had stopped to check out the car and caught us?"

She grinned. "*You'd* have some fancy explaining to do."

"Why me?"

"Because I would have fainted dead away from humiliation."

Joe flopped back in the seat and laughed. "Do you realize that I essentially live with my parents and you live with your grandmother. We're a couple of real sophisticates, Ell."

She started to chuckle, shedding the last remnants of embarrassment. Things definitely could have been worse.

A few minutes later, she got into her car and shut the door. Something fundamental had changed inside her tonight. She could sense it, and it had to do with Joe. She was still afraid to get involved with anyone, and yet she was filled with hope that she would.

With Joe.

• • •

The christening reception was in full swing, and Ellen gazed around the large drawing room from her spot in the buffet line. She had been afraid a christening would dredge up memories she might not be able to handle, but she had braced herself mentally. She knew she could be proud of herself for her composure.

Joe's parents' gothic-style home was every bit as palatial as her grandmother's, and the place was packed with Carlinis. Everyone smiled at her. Everyone was polite. Everyone acted pleased that she had come with Joe. And yet every so often she felt an underlying hostility. It was directed toward her.

She told herself that people did display a certain caution on first meeting. That was only natural—especially since her background was known. Nobody excluded her from a conversation. In fact, this was her first moment alone, and she had taken the opportunity to get some food. But she sensed a definite hostility from somewhere. It reminded her of something, but she couldn't quite put her finger on it.

Maybe it was she. There must be over a hundred people here, and the reception was as lavish as any she'd been to before, including ones in Europe. She admitted she had been expecting a more boisterous gathering, but these were sophisticated Americans, comfortable and knowledgeable in their wealth and power. She had wanted to make a good impression, but she wondered if she had blundered somewhere. She didn't think so. She'd been trained too well to make a faux pas now.

She looked over at Joe, who was momentarily trapped in a conversation with his father and two of his uncles. She forgot her anxiety as she gazed at him, memorizing the planes of his cheeks, his straight nose, his mobile lips. The intensity of his expression as he talked and gestured brought an unconscious smile to her. She knew she was gawking like a schoolgirl, but she couldn't stop herself. She was beginning to trust again. Trust her body, trust herself, and trust Joe. The past few days had been wonderful. And too darn platonic, she admitted with a wry smile. She sighed and smoothed down her blue-gray cashmere skirt.

She looked up in time to see Joe excuse himself and hurry over to her. He stood so close that she imagined she could feel every line and dip of his body. The people in the room seemed to slide into the distance.

"You'd better not smile like that," he said in a low voice. "Otherwise I won't be responsible for my actions."

"You'd shock your family," she pointed out, deciding he looked extremely handsome in his gray tweed suit.

"That's their problem," he said, grinning. "Hungry?"

"Starving." That was another thing. She was eating like a horse.

Joe's grin widened intimately, as if he were taking credit for that. Maybe he should, she decided. His father called to him, and he made a face as he waved back in acknowledgment.

"They're going to drive me crazy today. I'm sorry, Ell, but I'll only be a few more minutes, I promise."

She chuckled. "I'm fine."

He went off, muttering something about retirees who refused to retire. She watched him until he was in the center of the small knot of men, then reluctantly shifted her gaze from him.

She found herself being stared at by Joe's mother and two aunts whose names she couldn't remember. All three were seated on a sofa, their backs straight, their eyes narrowed. Their disapproval of her was unmistakable, and Ellen was stunned by it. Today was the first time she had met any of the three, but she knew with certainty she had been judged and sentenced already.

A similar scene rose from her past, and now she remembered why the underlying hostility seemed so familiar. Her former husband's mother and aunts had sat in just the same way, looked her over in just the same way, and judged her lacking in just the same way. They had fed Florian's whims with a vengeance against her, and interfered with the marriage at every turn.

Clearly, she was unacceptable yet again to another man's family. This time, though, she had headlines to precede her.

Realizing her hands were shaking, she clenched them into tight fists. She refused to let any hurt show and gazed back at the three older women for a long moment, then tilted her chin and turned away in a rebuff she'd learned from her grandmother. Her stomach was churning, any pleasure in the day gone. The last thing she wanted to do was eat, and she slipped out of line and headed for the closest quiet corner. To her relief she managed to find an unoccupied wingback chair along a wall. But she had no sooner sat down when she spotted Joe's sister Carol and Mario. Mario held two laden plates. As Ellen forced her composure into place, she realized she'd nearly forgotten about Mario and the recipe. She'd been too wrapped up in Joe.

"Here," Ellen offered, standing and stepping away from the chair. She nodded at Mario, then said to Carol, "I know it's only one, but take it, please."

"Go ahead, Carol," Mario said. "I can stand."

"Are you sure you don't mind?" Carol asked, looking harried.

Ellen smiled. "Not at all."

The other woman smiled back in gratitude and settled in the wing chair with a sigh. "The baby was up at dawn, the caterer forgot half the order, and my feet are killing me."

Ellen grinned. At least Joe's sister was friendly. "You look lovely. No one would know."

"You're so nice." Carol accepted the plate Mario handed her. "Thank you, Mario. I don't know where that husband of mine got to. Probably snuck into the study to watch the Phillies, the stinker, while I got the baby down for a nap. You've been a big help. And thanks for checking on those orders for me at the office. I hadn't realized how much I had let slip by me these past weeks."

Ellen could feel the hairs on her neck prickle. Carol held a quarter of the recipe. She was the one Joe trusted most. Mario glanced at her, then back at Carol.

"It was my pleasure," he said. "You know I'm glad to help you any way I can."

"I may just take you up on that," Carol said, digging her fork into a sizable helping of lasagna.

Mario smiled as he followed suit.

The prickles grew stronger as Ellen understood the scenario unfolding before her. Busy new mother and fast-paced executive with too many pressures trying to juggle it all. She could easily succumb to a pair of helping hands, and it wouldn't matter who they were attached to for the moment. Carol could make a misjudgment without realizing it at first. She could give away her part of the recipe by mistake. And Mario had to know that. Ellen's presence was hardly a deterrent. Right here, right in front of her, he was actually making a maneuver for the recipe.

Ellen forgot her previous hurt as her brain scrambled for a way to inject a warning. Joe must have told his sister about Mario. All she had to do was reinforce it.

"It's very nice to see you again, Mario," she began. Out of the corner of her eye, she noted Carol's gaze widen. She pressed on. "Thomas told me the other day at the plant about how much he enjoyed the Sinatra concert. He was so pleased that you had treated him."

Mario stared at her, his face devoid of all emotion. Somehow the lack of facial expression was frightening.

Ellen resisted the urge to run. Smiling as innocently as possible, she added, "I hope your mother wasn't too jealous."

He held her gaze for a moment longer, then said, "No."

Ellen nodded. Carol sat frozen in the chair now,

her food forgotten. Mario, after one glance at her, turned on his heel and walked away.

"Thank you," Carol said, looking up from her plate.

Ellen smiled genuinely this time. "That's okay. I'm glad I could help."

Her words echoed Mario's, and the two women burst into giggles. After the hostility from Joe's mother and aunts, it was nice to find a friend in Joe's sister.

"Mommy, Mommy!"

Ellen whirled around at the familiar, piping voice, expecting to see her son running full tilt toward her as he always did when he was excited. It was a little dark-haired boy running, but it wasn't Paulo. It would never be Paulo again.

Anguish shot through her, rooting her to the spot. She'd thought she was past this mistake. She'd prayed she was. Somehow she managed to turn, managed to plaster a smile on her face for Carol, who was frowning at her in puzzlement. She realized Carol hadn't seen her reaction to the child.

She shrugged, as if confused herself. "I thought I heard Joe calling me."

Carol's brow cleared, and Ellen knew she had covered her break. But that was all she had covered.

Today held too many sharp reminders of what she had lost.

And of what she couldn't have again.

"I thought I'd lost you."

Joe slipped an arm around Ellen's waist, pleased

to find her talking with his sister. She didn't lean into him, but he didn't expect her to.

"I'm stealing her away," he said pointedly to his sister, who smiled at him.

"I'm not surprised," Carol said. She turned to Ellen and added quietly, "Thank you again."

"You're welcome again," Ellen said, clearly understanding what Carol meant. "Good luck to you and the baby."

Joe steered Ellen into another, quieter part of the house, knowing they'd been at the christening long enough to satisfy familial obligations. Besides, if he didn't get out of there, his father and uncles would probably tackle him again about some aspect of the business.

"Ellen, you were supposed to be saving my place in the food line—"

"Would you mind taking me home, Joe?" she asked, breaking in.

"What?" he exclaimed, halting.

"Would you take me home, please?"

"But—"

"I have a migraine headache." Her voice was almost cold.

He stared at her, openmouthed. She did look pale and the lines around her mouth were tight with tension. But he could sense a desperation in her that had nothing to do with a headache. Any expression in her eyes was shuttered tight against him. The walls were back up, and higher than before. She was withdrawing from him, and he had no idea why.

"What's wrong, Ell?" he asked, putting his hands on her arm.

"I told you." She stepped away from him and wrapped her arms around her chest. "I have a migraine."

"You didn't have one ten minutes ago."

"I have one now. If you won't take me home, I'll call a cab."

"Ell—"

"Joe, please."

He set his jaw. "All right. I'll take you home."

He'd left her alone for ten lousy minutes, and he'd lost her.

Nine

"I don't think so, but thank you for asking."

Joe gripped the telephone receiver tighter at Ellen's overly polite words. This was the fourth time she had turned down a dinner invitation in as many days.

"Ell, why won't you tell me what's wrong?" he snapped, exasperated with her. He'd asked the question every time he'd called, and he felt like a broken record.

"Because nothing is." Her answer hadn't changed either.

He clenched his teeth together in an effort to rein in his temper. "All right. Mario is meeting someone again. The man from the rink, I think—"

"I'm sorry, Joe. But I'm afraid I can't help you any more. I haven't been much help anyway."

"Ellen—"

"I have to go. Thank you for calling, Joe."

"Ell! Don't hang—"

The click and the dial tone interrupted him as if on cue.

". . . up the phone," he finished. He stared at the telephone, tempted to slam down the receiver. He was really beginning to get aggravated with her. Controlling his temper, he very gently set the receiver into the cradle. He felt as if he were back to square one.

She sounded so blank that it scared him. He knew something had happened at the christening. Nothing else could explain her abruptly cutting him off. He'd talked to Carol, who had assured him that Ellen had been fine with her, right up until the moment he had joined them. In fact, no one else had spoken to Ellen, except Mario. And he hadn't spoken to her alone.

Restless, Joe stood up and started pacing his office. He couldn't understand it, yet the fact remained that as soon as Ellen had turned her back on his sister, the facade had crumbled. Who or what had sent her withdrawing into her shell?

"The answer to that question," he said aloud to the empty office, "is I don't know."

He ran his hand through his hair in frustration. She had been polite but quiet on the drive home. No amount of questioning or coaxing had budged her then. And it certainly hadn't worked since. At least her training in good manners was on his side, and she was coming to the telephone. He'd thought that if he didn't push her, she might thaw enough to talk to him.

At the rate he was going, though, he never would break through that tenacious politeness. Worse, she had refused to help with Mario. She had never refused to help him with the recipe before. Okay, so he had lied, and she might have realized that. He sensed that even if he had needed her help, though, she still would have said no. She was insuring he had no opening anywhere.

He wasn't giving up. A woman like Ellen came along only once in a lifetime—if a man was lucky. She had been hurt very badly and nobody could blame her for her withdrawal. But she had opened something inside him, and he couldn't turn it off now. Not and still be whole. He remembered all too well those moments in the car. They had haunted him ever since, and now he wanted to curse himself for being noble. Yet he knew he wouldn't. He was in love with Ellen Kitteridge. He had to be. No amount of lust would explain this.

He stared at the phone, tempted to call again but knowing it was futile. Maybe the telephone had been a mistake. Maybe he ought to go out there. He knew how to keep six hundred workers from striking, but he had no idea what to do about one tenacious woman.

He needed help.

His secretary opened the office door, and he looked up, annoyed with the interruption.

"You have a meeting in five minutes with advertising," she said.

"Right," he muttered in a near growl. His advertising people were pushing for a new outside firm to handle their account. They didn't like the last campaign that the old firm had conducted. Neither did he. But he was in no mood for a meeting. He was in no mood for business of any kind. Ellen had occupied his thoughts continually until he couldn't concentrate on Carlini Foods. In fact, he was beginning not to give a damn about the company. That was bad.

"Whatever it is, I didn't do it," his secretary said.

Joe chuckled reluctantly, his tension easing slightly. "I'm sorry. Advertising in five."

She nodded and pulled the door shut, leaving him alone again. He rifled through the papers on his desk, looking for the projection report.

Then his hands stilled. He'd received help before with Ellen from a person who knew her very well.

He picked up the telephone and pressed the button for his secretary. When she answered, he said, "Hold advertising until I'm off my private line."

He switched to the private line and mentally crossed his fingers as he rang the Kitteridge house again. One thing he'd noticed was that Ellen didn't answer the phone. Sure enough, the accented voice of the housekeeper announced, "Kitteridge residence."

"Lettice Kitteridge, please." He hoped the older woman would talk to him. She had before. "This is Joe Carlini."

There was a pause, then the woman acknowledged him. Poor thing was probably confused as hell, he thought wryly.

Suddenly a voice grated in his ear. "I was beginning to wonder when you'd talk to me, Joseph."

Joe sighed in relief.

•   •   •

As Ellen dressed for dinner, she admitted eating was the last thing she felt like doing. But her grandmother had demanded that she "snap out of it" before the Gladwyne Flower Society arrived for their bimonthly dinner meeting. She'd snapped all right, she thought. Snapped into reality.

Looking in the mirror at the dark circles under her eyes, she decided reality was taking its toll. Her days and nights had been a blur of numb memories from the past and the present. They had blended together, confirming her pain and her resolve. In the end, she knew that however much it hurt, she had done the right thing by breaking off her involvement with Joe. She hoped he would understand that. As hard as it was to turn away from him, she had done it. She had done what was best for both of them. The incidents at the christening had reminded her of how people who . . . cared could be hurt.

She gazed into the mirror one last time, then whirled away from her reflection. She hated to admit that she had taken to watching *Bull Durham* nightly in a ritual of self-inflicted torture. And she always took Joe's telephone calls. That was a torture she didn't need, yet she did it because she told herself the best way to discourage him was for him to hear it from her own lips. Still, she couldn't shake the feeling that she was punishing herself.

"Silly," she muttered out loud. And stupid, and dumb. No more, she decided, straightening her shoulders. No more movies or telephone calls. Certainly no more spying. Joe was too sexy and exciting. Just being with him had caused her blood to sizzle. More than sizzle. She had burned for him.

No longer would she veer from her quest for peace and quiet. She would go down to her grand-mother's committee dinner and sit through the endless bickering and gossip of the other women with a smile on her face. It was her one last form of self-torment.

As she walked down the back staircase and through the dining room, she decided that she'd go on vacation somewhere, maybe travel from place to place until she found a spot that suited her. Maybe she'd stay for a long time. . . .

All thoughts fled when she entered the drawing room. Her sight dimmed and her ears buzzed as she saw Joe standing by the mantelpiece.

She blinked, positive she was having a night-mare. She wasn't. Joe was ensconced in her grand-mother's house as if he lived there. Even as frantic questions ran through her brain, she still couldn't believe it was real.

"There you are, Ellen." Her grandmother's voice echoed in her head. "We were waiting dinner on you. You know everyone, of course."

She was dimly aware of someone taking her arm. She turned to find her grandmother smiling smugly at her. Lettice's grip, however, would have cut a steel pipe in half. It forced Ellen to stiffen her spine. She had a pretty good idea of who invited Joe to dinner.

"Yes, I've met everyone," she managed to say.

As she plastered a smile on her face and greeted the others, she remembered the committee con-sisted of the most influential matrons of Philadel-phia society. And they all were the worst gossips on the eastern seaboard. She also realized Lettice must have purposefully arranged for Joe to be at this dinner to insure the best behavior from her granddaughter.

She finally forced her gaze squarely to Joe's. Her first thought was that he looked powerful among her grandmother's dainty Chippendale furniture. Not out of place, for he possessed a self-assurance that came from experience, not family connections. She noted he was holding a drink in one hand, and he was relaxed and comfortable with the gaggle of older women in the room. In fact, he seemed to thrive on their attention.

As she was led to his side, she found her tidbit of courage nearly deserting her. His smile was triumphant, and his gaze raked her body as he stepped toward her.

"Hello, Ell," he said softly.

She was forced to offer her hand. Even though she'd braced herself for the familiar response to his closeness, she was still unprepared for the shock that bolted through her at his touch. It was the other women leaning forward in their seats with great interest that kept her from throwing herself into his arms. She pulled her hand away, and in the crispest tone she could muster she said, "Joe. How nice to see you again. I didn't know you would be here tonight."

Her grandmother rushed in with an explanation. "He's making a wonderful donation to the society's fund-raiser next week, and we wanted to discuss the presentation with him."

"How lovely," Ellen commented. Whispering, she added for her grandmother's benefit, "I'll never forgive you for this."

"In a pig's eye you won't," her grandmother whispered back. Overhearing, Joe grinned at the two of them.

Louder, Lettice said, "We're having crowned roast of pork for dinner. Your favorite, Ellen. Joseph, will you escort Ellen into the dining room? The rest of us will follow."

Ellen gritted her teeth and refused to allow any reaction to show. Those old biddies were eyeing her like vultures watching a potential meal stagger along the desert floor, she thought in disgust. Joe's presence was enough to send their tongues wagging already, and she was not about to add fuel to the fire.

Dinner was a nightmare of polite conversation and underlying sensuality. Joe was seated across from her. He was charming and attentive to Philadelphia's most influential matriarchs. And every time he turned to her, she became a gazelle frozen in the sight of a big cat. She couldn't look away or stop her body from reacting to the proximity of his. Her brain insisted on replaying every intimate moment they'd shared. Her breasts ached and her thighs shifted restlessly of their own accord. She found herself watching his hands . . . and remembering the magic they created.

Somehow she managed to pick at enough food so that people might think she was dieting rather than suffering a loss of appetite. She doubted, though, that she was fooling anyone, least of all Joe. When the meal had ended and she could gracefully excuse herself, she was determined to escape as quickly as possible. Her grandmother, however, had other ideas.

"Ellen, you and Joseph must be bored to death with all this planning for the festival," Lettice said in a very innocent tone. "It's a beautiful night, so why don't you two take a walk in the back garden."

"Grandmother—"

"I'm very proud of my garden, Joseph," Lettice continued, squelching Ellen's protest before it had begun. "And I know you're interested in gardens. You were just telling us before dinner about your own grandmother's garden. I think you'll enjoy a little tour."

"I think I would, thank you." Joe nodded as he captured Ellen's gaze. The expression on his face was closed, and the lack of visible emotion made Ellen even more nervous.

"Lettice has a wonderful lighting system," one of the women said.

Another chimed in. "The fountain lights are the centerpiece. You can't appreciate the entire night display without it."

"Shall we go?" Joe asked, setting his napkin next to his plate and rising. He gazed at her expectantly.

Ellen sensed her grandmother's triumphant delight and knew she had been outmaneuvered. She rose from the table. As they left the room, the others launched into a discussion of the garden's creator.

"Jessica Brannen did a wonderful job for you, Lettice."

"Mikaris now, Margery. She got married again, remember? She does do wonderful work. Maybe we could get her for the festival. . . ."

Without a word, Ellen led Joe through the French

doors. Once they were outside, she marched down the path toward the fountain. "Don't dawdle, Joe, if you want to see grandmother's amazing garden."

"Ell, we need to talk."

"No time for it," she snapped, practically running along the path. She was angry at being manipulated into seeing him, but she also didn't trust herself to be alone with him. "You wanted the tour, so here are the azaleas, the mountain laurel, and the rhododendron. There are the yews and the boxwoods and the grass."

He kept pace with her. "Ellen, hold it—"

"Can't." They reached the fountain, and she was gratified to see Joe gape at the floodlit alabaster mermaids rising from the center of the water. The lights sent prisms of rainbows twinkling across the fountain.

Ellen took advantage of his momentary lapse of attention. She slipped across another path and through a planned gap in the bushes, then ran down the short slope of the lawn to the cabana by the swimming pool. Breathless, she took the spare key from under the mat and unlocked the door, determined to get away from Joe.

She had no sooner turned around to shut the cabana door when a hand pushed it wide open. She shrieked and backed away, putting the dust-covered sofa and chairs in the one-room building between her and him.

Joe shut the door behind him, and the click of the lock was a gunshot in the charged silence. He turned on the lights and surveyed the surroundings. "Clever of you to find us a private place to talk, Ell."

"We talked already. On the telephone, every day," she reminded him, forcing away her anxiety. "I told you, I'm not interested in having dinner with you, and I can't help you any longer with Mario."

"What happened on Sunday to change you?" he asked, coming around the left end of the furniture. "Why won't you tell me?"

She moved to her left, knowing she had to keep the furniture between them. "I . . . I realized that I wasn't interested any longer. I'm sorry I didn't make myself more clear."

"You were interested the night I took you back to your car," he reminded her, circling around the furniture. "Your mouth was interested, and your hands were all over me with interest. You moaned your interest—"

"Stop it!" she exclaimed. Images that matched his words ran through her head.

"You promised to be patient," he said, his gaze steady on her. "But you ran again. I know something happened at the christening to make you run. Tell me—"

"I told you already!" Her head was pounding with the twin devils of fear and need. He was relentlessly pursuing her around the room, and the faster she dodged one way, the quicker he shifted the other. She didn't know if she was managing to keep out of his reach . . . or if he was allowing her to. She tried again to persuade him to give up on her. "I have no interest in being involved with you. What's between us is just a physical attraction, chemistry if you will, and that's all it is."

"Really?" He shed his suit jacket and laid it over

the back of a chair as he went by. His fingers began to work on his tie.

"What the hell are you doing?" she demanded, stumbling over her feet. She caught her balance before she fell.

"Getting physical."

"You can't!" Her brain scrambled for a further protest as the tie joined the jacket. Instead her gaze was drawn to his hands flicking the open buttons of his shirt, revealing the swath of dark, silky hair on his chest.

He smiled knowingly at her. "Yes, I can. Why not find out for sure if this is just some good old-fashioned lust? Or are you afraid to find out it's not?"

Stalking her again, he undid his cuff links. She watched in fascination, her steps unconsciously slowing, as he peeled the shirt from his body and dropped it over a lamp. His shoulders were broad, and the hair on his upper chest arrowed down past his waistband, drawing the eye to the trimly muscled torso.

Her mouth went dry. She wanted desperately to touch him. She knew she would be lost if she did. But it was more than physical, and she knew it. The thought terrified her.

She ducked behind the sofa. "Joe, why can't you just let it go? Just write me off as any other man would."

His hands stilled at his belt buckle and he stared at her. "But you're not any other woman. And I'm not any other man. Chemistry is for labs, Ell. I'm in love with you."

"No!" She froze, the words swirling through her brain.

He halted his pursuit. "That's what you're really afraid of, isn't it? That's what made you turn away as you have. Love. You love me."

It couldn't be true, she thought dimly. It wasn't possible. After her first marriage and the loss of her son, she should be immune to love. "I . . . I can't."

"You can't. Not you *don't*." He was directly across from her. He braced his hands on the sofa back and leaned forward. His eyes were blazing, forcing her to remain still. "Not you don't, Ell. Say it."

She clamped her lips shut against a further giveaway. She couldn't say it, wouldn't acknowledge the truth. Their wrangling before had had an element of anticipation, but now she was being smothered by his demand. She raced for the door and escape. He was there before her, his arms embracing her. She knew she had been truly trapped.

"Say it," he demanded.

"I love you," she shouted. "Now let me go!"

"Never." His mouth found hers in a scorching kiss.

When he finally lifted his head, she slumped against him in defeat. The warmth of his bare skin against her cheek was like a drug she craved. The musk of cologne and male enveloped her senses. She hated herself for being weak.

"I'm not good enough for you," she whispered, remembering the looks of disapproval from his mother and aunts. "I never will be, and I won't do that to you."

"Nobody is finer than you, Ellen Kitteridge," he said, stroking her hair. "Nobody."

His lips found hers again. She was pressed along the length of his body, aware of every inch of him. Potent need was suddenly pounding through her, catching her by surprise as it always did. She knew she should be fighting this, but she couldn't find the willpower. And knowing she loved him left her defenseless. As her tongue entwined with his, she knew it was more than attraction that had drawn them together. Warmth and light flooded to the center of her. She never felt more alive than when she was with him. What she had lost could never be replaced, but what he offered was a different beginning. A beginning she could no longer deny.

Then her emotions gave way to a primitive longing, and their mouths pressed together feverishly. She ran her hands along his shoulders, feeling the flesh and bone and muscle bunch and move under her fingers. Her blood pulsed heavily through her veins. His hand cupped her breast, and she moaned at the ache he created.

His lips left hers to trail kisses down her throat, and he chanted her name as if it were a litany. When he opened her blouse and unhooked her bra, she pressed her freed breasts into his chest. The feel of skin against skin perfectly matched drove her beyond redemption.

"I love you," she murmured, burying her fingers in his hair. "I love you."

He kissed first one nipple, then the other. "I know."

He lifted her in his arms and strode the few paces to the sofa. Then she was beneath him, their bodies straining together as their passion overrode any thought of restraint. The limited space of the sofa was barely a hindrance.

For the first time, they were alone in a place that offered the opportunity and the means to make love without interruption. The knowledge heightened her awareness, and she wondered if she had unconsciously fled to the cabana for this. It didn't really matter. Their lovemaking was inevitable. From the moment she had first looked into his eyes, she had been captured by fate.

She forgot everything as she helped him shed the rest of their clothes. They both gasped at the touch of their bodies now devoid of barriers. Ellen thought she would die, her need pushed to even greater heights. Joe's hands and mouth left no part of her untouched. It was as if he already knew every pleasure point she possessed. He rose on his knees, her legs draped over his thighs. Instead of feeling vulnerable, she felt invincible. He leaned forward and gently took a nipple between his lips. His tongue swirled around the sensitive nub until she was writhing in pleasure. He raised his head and smiled at her, then his fingers found her moistness. She cried out and dug her nails into his shoulders as he stroked her to a frenzy.

Joe clenched his teeth against the desire rapidly overtaking him. From the beginning, his imagination had tormented him with visions of making love to Ellen. And they all were pale imitations to the true feel of her in his arms, the way she moved under his hands. Her thighs shifted restlessly, tormenting him with their silkiness. Her hands guided his lips to her breasts, the nipples straining at the touch of his tongue. She was incredible in her response to him, and she was driving his need out of control. It would be too easy to take her in passion. He wanted, instead, to take her in love.

But her hands glided down his back and around his hips, drawing him forward to her. She enclosed him in the heat he had created, and then they were moving together in endless obsession. He was lost in her, and he never wanted to return. She made him feel whole and unconquerable. Complete, he thought dimly. She made him feel complete. He would not take from her, but give as she gave to him. When she convulsed beneath him, he held her tightly to protect her from the forces raging inside her. But his own urgings overwhelmed him and he joined her in the tender storm. It faded into love's calm peace.

Long minutes later, he became aware of cool air against his naked back. The dust sheet had somehow tangled around his feet. Ellen lay beneath him quietly, as if she were too weighted to move. But she had said she loved him. He smiled into her shoulder, at first happy. Then he realized how he had had to force the confession from her.

He lifted his head and shifted his weight onto his elbows. Swallowing back his fear, he said, "Ell . . . I don't know what to say . . . I forced you."

He watched her eyes slowly open. Incredibly, she smiled at him. "No, you didn't."

"Yes, I did. I should never have forced you to say 'I love you.' I'm sorry, so sorry."

She chuckled, her voice lazy with spent passion. "I think I trapped myself into this."

"No—"

"Joe. I'm scared to death you'll discover you made a terrible mistake with me. Don't make it worse by being a gentleman."

"I'll shut up," he promised. "And you're the best mistake I ever made, okay?"

She nodded, then her eyes widened. "Omigod! I forgot about the vultures."

"The vultures?"

"Grandmother's guests. I can't go back in there and face them after . . ."

"Then we won't." He stretched out alongside her, then pulled her on top of him. "I'm sure your grandmother will have a plausible excuse for them."

Ellen's eyes were bright with amusement and something more. Something he knew was only for him. "I think the two of you planned this."

He cupped her breast as he considered the question. "Not quite this."

He ran his finger across her blossoming nipple and watched her eyes slowly close. Her breathing quickened. She had always responded to his touch, as he had to hers, as if they were finely tuned to each other.

"Your grandmother definitely didn't plan this," he murmured, his own breath becoming more rapid.

Ellen grinned. "Don't bet on it. You don't know my grandmother."

The "vultures" were long gone when Ellen finally climbed the stairs to her room. Night was fading, and the early morning sun was slowly lighting the dark sky. The house was quiet, and she was surprised her grandmother wasn't up to "check" on her. She couldn't stop smiling as contentment and weariness wove through every corner of her body.

Once inside her room, she found she was too tired to sleep, and she curled, instead, into a stuffed armchair. She sat for long minutes, feeling the lazy satisfaction in every inch of her and remembering how it had come there. On the small, round table next to the chair was a boudoir lamp, and she sighed and turned it on. A picture of a small boy caught her eye. She lifted it, her fingers caressing the silver frame. She had shut herself away for such a long time out of grief . . . and out of guilt. Despite what had happened in the cabana tonight, it would be easy to remember the pain of a bad marriage and a lost child and crawl back in her shell again.

She was still afraid of being hurt, but tonight she had lost the battle against Joe. She knew if she truly trusted her heart she would find what she really wanted—what Joe was offering. All she had to do was stop looking back.

She held the picture for a moment longer, then smiled and set it aside. From now on, she would look forward.

Ten

"And where are you going?"

Ellen eyed her grandmother for a long moment, then picked up her purse. "Out to lunch."

"With Joseph." It was a statement, rather than a question.

Ellen didn't answer. Her grandmother had been too darn smug over the "garden tour" that had taken place two nights ago. Last night, when Joe had arrived to take her to dinner, Lettice had been grinning like a matchmaker who had just pulled off the coup of the century. A little suspense wouldn't hurt, Ellen decided, and it might just teach Lettice not to interfere. Or at least not to gloat when she did.

"Ellen, are you or are you not going out to lunch with Joseph?"

She shrugged. "I thought I'd do a little shopping too. Do you need anything?"

"An answer!" Lettice snapped, her impatience getting the best of her.

"We'll see."

Ellen glanced in the foyer mirror for one last look before she left the house. Why is it, she wondered, that a person could look great upstairs, but not downstairs? Now she decided Joe would probably hate her mint green silk shirtwaist. Then the knowing smile hovering on her lips caught her attention and she forgot the dress. She did and yet didn't look any different. She was floating half the time, and the other half she was worried about the disapproval she'd sensed in some of his family members. She would have to be reassured by his actions. Lunch today at the Carlini Foods company dining room would be the test.

Love was confusing. . . .

"Ellen! I demand to know—"

"Good-bye, Grandmother," she said, turning away from her reflection. She'd be very late if she changed. Besides, she'd been through her closet twice and this was her best dress. Remembering her manners, she added, "You have a nice lunch, too."

"Ellen Kitteridge, you haven't said a word about Joseph since the other night."

Stopping on the threshold, Ellen turned and smiled. "You like him, don't you?"

"Yes." The fire of battle was in the silver-haired woman's eyes. "The least you could do is thank me for the other night, missy."

"In a pig's eye." Ellen shut the front door on her grandmother's gasp of outrage.

She grinned.

• • •

Joe glanced at the desk clock and sighed with relief when he saw the time. Ellen would be here any minute for lunch. The company dining room was not his first choice, but he had so much work to catch up on that he hadn't been sure he could get away from the plant.

He smiled, admitting to himself that if he took her some place cozy for lunch, he would never come back. Dinner had been a close call last night. Actually, they'd done pretty well at keeping their hands off each other, considering they had made love just twenty-four hours before that. He remembered looking at her, sensing the same longing in her as was in him, and cursing the fates that they had no privacy. It was finally time to move out of the Wynnewood family home. Granted, his parents traveled a good deal. Unfortunately, they weren't traveling at the moment.

"Where did you take a woman before?" Ellen had asked, desire clear in her eyes.

She hadn't liked his answer of "her place or a hotel." Ellen was too fine to take to a hotel. Besides, they hadn't had much of a courtship, and he was determined to give her that. He had sensed it wasn't so much the "where" that bothered her, but that a place had been found at all. Still, he loved the thought that she was jealous, even though she had nothing to be jealous about. It was a good sign that he was getting past the last of her barriers. Making love had resolved her emotions for him. What it had resolved for him was unbelievable. Much as it would torture him, he knew it was better that they didn't make love again for a while. Their relationship needed time to cement the emotional foundations. He sensed that once that was secure, their physical relationship could only be heightened.

"It'll probably kill me," he muttered, deciding he'd have a smile on his face when he went.

He looked down at his now neglected paperwork and groaned. He had to stop daydreaming like this.

Someone tapped on his back office door that led directly to a hallway. Surprised, he rose and unlocked it.

His cousin, Jamie Carlini, stood in the empty corridor. "Are you alone, Joe?"

He nodded, and Jamie came into the office. After the door was shut again, Jamie pulled a long envelope from his breast pocket.

"It's my resignation," he said.

Joe gaped at him. "Resignation? What . . . why—"

"I had an anonymous phone call," Jamie said, his normally tanned complexion sallow. "I . . . I haven't been faithful to my wife. I thought I was hiding it very well, that no one would find out. But apparently someone has. He didn't ask for anything. Not yet. I've thought about this, and I had to admit just how vulnerable I really am to such an attack. I know pressure can be applied. A lot of pressure. I thought a resignation and confession were the best way to handle it. If you'll come to my bank, I'll turn over my part of the recipe straight from my safety deposit box."

Joe stared at his cousin, then at the envelope held out to him. Anger shot through him at this latest and nastiest twist to Mario's game. "Make three guesses who your anonymous caller is. And the first two don't count."

Jamie set his jaw. "It wasn't hard to figure out. When you first told me about Thomas being approached, it went through my head that I might be vulnerable. But I've been so careful about the affair—"

"Not careful enough," Joe snapped, not having any sympathy for Jamie. Jamie's wife, Karen, was a lovely woman, and she adored her husband. "You should have told me about this before. We might have been able to handle it without the affair coming out."

"I don't know how anyone found out."

"Someone did."

"She was . . . exciting. But it was stupid," Jamie said. "All around stupid."

Joe took the envelope and crumpled it up. "Resigning won't solve the problem. Your 'anonymous' caller might just let your secret out in revenge, because you took yourself out of the play."

Jamie curled his hands into fists. "I realize that. I've already told Karen. I don't know if I have a marriage left."

Joe shook his head at the hurt that must have caused. "Then you've spiked his guns at the expense of your marriage. This has gone too far. It's past time that I ask for someone else's resignation and to hell with the family."

Jamie looked wide-eyed at him. "Joe, I can't say it was Mario on the telephone. The voice was too muffled."

"I don't care about proof. I've had enough." His

temper got the better of him. "If there's trouble, then there's trouble. Maybe everyone will finally wise up and realize this is a business. But Mario is not ruining anyone else's life. This will stop today."

"Joe—"

"No. My job is to protect this company. And it's about time I do my job."

His intercom line rang. He picked up the receiver. "No calls—"

"Ms. Kitteridge is here."

"Ask her to wait a moment." He set the receiver down and turned to Jamie. He thrust the envelope back into his cousin's hands. "As they say in the old country: You have honor, James Carlini. It took a lot of courage to resign, but you're too damn good a lawyer to lose. The company needs you."

"Thank you," Jamie said in a low voice.

Joe patted his shoulder. "Don't worry about Mario. I'll remove his fangs for good."

"Watch you don't get bitten in the process," Jamie warned.

Joe nodded.

After Jamie had left the office by the private door, Joe stood for a moment, then shook his head at Jamie's foolishness. He crossed the oriental rug and opened the door to his secretary's office. At the sight of Ellen's smile, he set aside the thought of a confrontation with Mario. Once she was in his office, the door safely shut against curious eyes, he pulled her into his arms for a hungry kiss.

"You certainly know how to say 'hello,' " she said, breathless when he finally let her go.

"Glad you like it," he murmured, smoothing his hands down her back. He loved the feel of her skin under the mint green silk dress. And he loved the dress. Her skin was glowing. "I was almost afraid you wouldn't come."

"I was almost afraid I wouldn't either," she admitted.

"I would have come after you."

"That's what I figured." She smiled, then frowned. "What's wrong?"

He dropped his hands away. "How did you know?"

"You look pressured."

He told her about Jamie's resignation, his anger returning.

"I should have fired Mario long ago," he finished, slicing the air with one hand. "It's gone too far now."

"Maybe we should postpone our lunch," she suggested.

"No," he said, forcing himself to calm down. "I'm just sorry we have to have it here."

"No, we don't," she said eagerly. "There's a Burger King just down the road."

He chuckled. "Ellen! You, at a fast-food restaurant? Somebody better call the society columnists."

"Anybody ever tell you you're a snob, Joe?" she asked, herding him out the door.

Eventually Joe found himself sitting at an orange laminate table looking across at a former princess.

"I bet Prince Charles doesn't chow down on a

whopper," he said, as he watched Ellen do exactly that.

She grinned at him. "He doesn't know what he's missing."

"I love you, Ell."

She set the burger down and gazed at him, her eyes brimming with warmth. "I never thought I would hear those words in a Burger King. Watch you don't get mayonnaise on your tie."

"Yes, my love. By the way, thanks for paying."

"I figured I better. You had a free meal planned, Mr. Last of the Big-Time Spenders."

He needed this, he thought. He wondered if she had any idea how she affected him. She was a well in which he would always find renewal. The image of her in the cabana ran through his head, and he pushed it away. He couldn't afford to torture himself. Right after lunch, he would solve the Mario problem for good, then the company would be back to normal and he could concentrate on wooing Ellen. Everything was finally coming together for him. And for her.

But the easiness of lunch was lost the moment they returned to Carlini Foods. Mario was pulling into his parking space, just as Ellen maneuvered her car into one of the spaces reserved for visitors.

Joe's anger returned twofold, and he scrambled out of Ellen's car as she braked to a halt. He'd have it out with Mario right here. He hated the thought of the traitor setting foot in the building again.

"Stay here, Ell," he said. Then he strode across the lot, catching Mario as the latter climbed out of his car.

"You just resigned from the company," Joe informed him, grabbing hold of the Corvette's door before it swung shut. He opened it wider. "Get back in the car and get out."

Mario's mouth opened in astonishment. "What?"

"You're resigning from Carlini Foods," Joe repeated. "I won't tolerate your presence in the building again. Now get out."

"Why would I resign?" Mario asked, his brows drawing together in puzzlement.

"For trying to sell out the company." Joe stared him down until Mario broke eye contact.

"You have no proof of that."

Joe smiled grimly. "Let's just say you better start worrying if your voice was recognized. Jamie's no longer a candidate for future blackmail tactics, and you are no longer employed by this company. It's over, Mario. I don't care what you say officially, but you're out. Now."

"I have no idea what you're talking about."

But Mario's eyes had narrowed and his lips had thinned the moment Joe had mentioned Jamie's name. The expression of frustration was unmistakable.

"Liar," Joe said softly. "Take the chance I'm offering you, cousin. You've made too many mistakes already. You tried to sell out your own relatives."

"You don't have any proof. You won't get it past the family—"

"Don't bet the farm on that, pal. If you fight me on this, your betrayal will come out. Thomas, Carol, and Jamie can back me. And Ellen witnessed your little chat with the man at the rink. What company is he from?"

No answer.

"The circumstantial evidence is building up against you," Joe went on. "Enough to make most people very suspicious of your actions lately. I've kept this contained so far among the parties involved. You can save your own and your parents' dignity at least with the resignation—"

"I'll take you down, Joe," Mario snarled.

Joe stared at him coolly, unimpressed by the threat. "You're like a little kid who's just had his toy taken away from him. The recipe's a lost cause. It always has been. Your verbal resignation is effective immediately. I want your written resignation delivered to my office before the day is out. I'll be cleaning out your desk personally, and I'll have your things sent to you. You can't do anything else and you know it."

Mario stared at him, his eyes filled with hatred. His jaws were clamped so tightly together, Joe wondered if they would shatter. Finally, Mario climbed back into the car. Joe slammed the door shut behind him. He watched as Mario brought the engine to screaming life, then backed the sports car out of the slot, the back tires squealing from abuse. The brakes screeched once again, then the car roared out of the lot.

Joe took a deep breath and relaxed. It was done. He hoped Mario would just cut his losses and give some innocuous reason for leaving the company. The man had enough pride to do that rather than risk showing his stupidity to others. At least he hadn't taken one last bite, Joe thought, remembering Jamie's warning. He'd been more worried about that than he cared to admit.

Ellen was walking across the lot, and he walked toward her. They met in the middle.

"Your cousin took the rest of the afternoon off, I see," she said, concern in her blue-green eyes. "Permanently?"

Joe nodded. He put his arm around her and pulled her close to his side.

"Will he cause trouble over this?" she asked.

"I don't know, but I don't see him exposing his pride to a possible downfall. The stunt with the spice suppliers and now Jamie's blackmail were two big mistakes on his part. He'd have to do some very fast talking to make his actions sound innocent at this point." He was surprised that his cousin had gone with so little fight. It made him wonder what he would find in Mario's desk.

"I think I'll miss playing *I Spy* with Mario and the mysterious stranger," she said, leaning lightly against him.

He chuckled. "If you behave yourself, I'll take you back to Atlantic City this weekend."

Her breasts were pressed against his side, her hips touching his flank. He could almost trace her torso with his own. Her long legs brushed along his. His blood heated at the unconscious caress of feminine curves. He had been joking, of course, but now the idea sounded better and better.

"I've always had a fondness for Atlantic City," she murmured.

"Maybe," he whispered, leaning over and nibbling her ear, "I'll take you now."

"Oh, no, you won't." She smiled and stepped away. "One of us better be sensible."

"Ell . . ." he began, walking toward her.

"Go back to work, Joe."

"I hate sensible," he muttered, shoving his hands in his pockets.

She laughed. "Go to work."

"See you tonight?"

"My grandmother wouldn't have it any other way. Come for dinner."

He grinned.

Finally, life was on track.

Eleven

"It's a shame we can't go swimming."

From their balcony vantage point high above the beach, Ellen looked out over the ocean and sighed. She hadn't realized how much she had been anticipating Joe's promised weekend in Atlantic City. Even though the sun shone brightly over the resort, the temperature was still too cool for a dip in the water. That was the only disappointment.

Hands grasped her shoulders and spun her around into a devastating kiss. She was amused for a moment, then the feel of his mouth locked to hers overtook her. Wrapping her arms around his neck, she gladly mated her tongue with his.

"Remind me to kiss you like that when we're on the boardwalk," Joe said after he finally lifted his head. "I owe you one."

She had no idea what he was talking about, but

she nodded anyway. She was not about to pass up another kiss like that.

She slipped out of his arms and went back into the luxurious bedroom. "You didn't tell me you rented a beachfront condo in Atlantic City."

"That's because I bought it."

She whirled around in astonishment, and he grinned at her.

"It's amazing what you can buy on a moment's notice," he added. "This place is completely furnished, with all the amenities of a hotel. Now we can come here any time we want to play *I Spy*."

"You're getting kinky in your old age," she said, shaking her head and turning back into the bedroom, intent on unpacking her bag.

Instead, she found herself being tossed on the bed. Joe came down on top of her.

"I'll show you old age."

"Don't forget the kinky."

"Right."

Later, she lay in his arms, lazy with satisfaction. She didn't want to know what the future held. She was content just to be here like this with Joe. Her mind, however, dredged up the memory of his mother and aunts glaring at her. She forced it away, not wanting anything to intrude on the moment. It returned, and she shifted restlessly away from Joe.

"Watch where you're putting that knee," he said in a high, piping voice.

Realizing how close she had come to unmanning him, she flushed, then giggled. "Sorry."

"That's better. Where were you going anyway?" he asked.

"Nowhere, really. I was just getting more comfortable." She settled back down against him, pulling the sheet up over their bodies.

"I think we'll spend the weekend here," he said, stroking her arm.

She thought about the three disapproving faces. They might not like her, but she'd be a fool to give up Joe without a fight. Determination flooded through her. She wouldn't worry until she had good reason to, she decided.

"I think I like that idea."

He rolled on top of her and smiled wolfishly. "Sex maniac."

She pressed her thighs to his. "Looks like my knee missed by a wide margin."

"Thank your lucky stars."

She burst into laughter at the drop in his voice.

He nuzzled her ear, then said, "Will you stop laughing so we can make love?"

She abruptly sobered, although one last giggle escaped her lips.

"That's better."

He leaned down to kiss her when the telephone rang.

"What the . . ." He sat up as it rang again. "I knew I should have waited to have the phone installed."

"That's what you get for being a conscientious company executive," she said, rolling onto her side. The muscles of his back intrigued her, and she began to trace them with her fingers.

"The entire plant had better be exploding," he said, snatching the receiver.

Ellen frowned as Joe's voice went from anger to frustration to restrained rage. She couldn't tell what the problem was from his clipped answers, but she knew it was serious. Leaving off her play, she sat up next to him and wound the sheet across her body.

Joe didn't crash the receiver down. Instead, his movements were deliberate, almost slow. Ellen held her breath, realizing he was so angry he was afraid to express it.

"I'm sorry, Ell," he finally said, his expression stony. "That was my father. An emergency meeting of the board of Carlini Foods has been called for tomorrow afternoon."

"This is about your firing Mario, isn't it?"

He nodded, and she put her arms around him. "You did the right thing, Joe."

"I know." He held her tightly. "Much as I was hoping to, I didn't think I'd avoid this. Mario's taking quite a chance with his pride."

"We'll go back now," she said. "That will give you time to prepare."

"I'll need you tomorrow."

Part of her wanted to refuse. She hated confrontations, and this would clearly be a family one.

"Of course," she said, overcoming her reluctance. Joe needed her.

Less than twenty-four hours later, she was wishing she'd heeded her common sense. She never felt more like an intruder as she listened to the wrangling among the family members in the conference room at the Carlini Foods executive offices.

Worse, she'd been accompanied by her grandmother. Lettice, when she had been told why her
granddaughter had returned and where she was
going, had insisted on coming too. No amount of
logic, pleading, or shouting had moved the woman
from her stance of "You need moral support, my
dear. You, too, Joseph." Lettice had bullied her
way into the company boardroom, protests glared
down by the "regal eye." Even Joe's mother had
been cowed. Both Ellen and her grandmother were
now seated near the door, away from the table.

Support was one thing, Ellen thought as she
glanced at her grandmother, who was avidly leaning forward to catch every word. Gleeful enjoy-
ment was quite another. She sighed. Her grandmother was outrageous sometimes.

Ellen shifted in her chair, again resisting the
urge to bolt. Joe had already explained his rea-
sons for firing Mario, with Thomas, Carol, and
Jamie backing him. Joe's father was the chair-
man, and he had held the meeting in tight rein.
The thirteen board members were clearly torn.
Their reactions ranged from suspicion, to disbelief, to tears. Ellen understood now why Joe had
been so adamant about proof against his cousin.
Mario, so far, hadn't said a word. His face was
blank of all expression. That worried her.

". . . as you can see, I had no choice in the
matter," Joe said, finishing his side of the story.
"I felt a resignation was the only way to keep the
recipe safe. Had Mario not been a family member
I would have fired him at first suspicion. I
felt I must give him every chance. I'm sorry, Aunt

Mary, Uncle Michael. I wish you never had to hear this."

"But Mario would never sell out the family!" Mario's mother wailed. Mario's father was grim-faced.

"Of course I wouldn't," Mario said smoothly. "It's true that I've run up a few debts—"

Many of the others grumbled their disagreement.

"More than a few," Mario conceded. "And my parents have cut off further funding. The family knows all this. But the idea that I would sell the recipe is ridiculous. I took Uncle Thomas to the Sinatra show because I wanted to pay him back for helping me with my department figures for the last quarter."

"I . . ." Thomas frowned. "I did go over them with the boy, that's true."

"That's why I took Thomas and not my mother." Mario grinned. "Sorry, Mom. As for Carol, I only offered to help her, knowing she has her hands full with the new baby. Anyone would do that, wouldn't they? I don't know anything about Jamie's *anonymous* phone call, but I feel bad for him. I'm sorry about the mix-up with the spicers. I had only wanted to try something new that might save the company some money. . . ."

He spoke very convincingly, and Ellen had a bad feeling that the majority of the stockholders might be swayed to Mario's side. Mario had a little smirk of tolerance every time he looked at Joe, as if he seemed to recognize the same thing. How Joe held his temper, she didn't know.

"If that boy is the angel he makes himself out to

be," Lettice whispered to Ellen, "then I have a bridge to sell these people."

"Shh!" Ellen glared at her grandmother. Unfortunately, Lettice was probably right.

". . . I think maybe Joe has been working too hard," Mario continued. "He's been under a lot of pressure lately—"

"You haven't explained why you were at the skating rink that morning," Joe interrupted, his voice surprisingly calm. "I've already explained how I picked up one of the phones in the plant and overheard a meeting being set up over the sale of the recipe for Mama's Homestyle, how you were the one I followed to the rink, and how Ellen witnessed you talking with a man. You're conveniently skipping over that part."

Mario looked pained. He glanced down at the table and rubbed his finger back and forth along its dark, highly polished surface. Finally he raised his head.

"I was trying to avoid this, but I see I have no choice." He straightened in his chair. "I *was* approached anonymously to sell the recipe."

Family members gasped.

"I, of course, would never do such a thing—"

Lettice gave an unladylike snort. Ellen silently agreed.

"—but I thought it best to discover what company was behind that offer and stop it before they could approach anyone else. So I pretended to be interested and agreed to meet the contact person at the rink." Mario shook his head. "But no one approached me there. Ellen was . . . mistaken, shall we say."

Ellen's stomach rolled with a strange tension.

Mario's solemnity increased. "After I was fired, I did a little checking around. I thought the other side figured out I was a ringer and that's why they didn't show. Now I think their contact person at the rink recognized Joe and saw a bigger and better opportunity to get the recipe. Someone else in this room was at the rink that day."

Everyone in the room gasped again in shock. Ellen froze in horror.

". . . someone whose own father owns substantial shares in a certain food conglomerate from Battle Creek, Michigan. Someone who's been trying to romance her way to the recipe."

The room was stunned into silence.

"How dare you accuse Ellen!" Lettice said in a threatening voice.

Ellen laid a hand on her grandmother's arm, silencing her. She rose from her chair. Shaking with her own anger, she gazed from person to person and saw the varying shades of belief under the surprise. Then she looked at Joe. His expression reflected his astonishment . . . and doubt.

Pain shot through her as he looked away. How could he believe his cousin? But she knew he must. She refused to defend herself. She had done nothing to defend. Without a word, she turned and walked out of the board room.

Joe was staring at his relatives in disbelief. How could they believe what Mario had said about Ellen? Yet he could see the frowns and sage nods at Mario's words. At the same moment, the boardroom door slammed shut behind Ellen, and he realized she had seen the same things he had. He shoved his chair back with a crash and ran after her, as the room again returned to life.

"My son is innocent!"

"In a pig's eye!"

"Joe! Joe!"

Joe slammed the heavy door against the din of voices and gavel-banging. He ignored it all, knowing he had to catch Ellen. She must be hurting badly. His mother had made a comment or two about Ellen which had bordered on the negative, but he had shrugged them away as her just being a fussy mother. He wished now he'd immediately vocalized his disbelief of Mario's accusation, not sat silently gaping. He'd been warned about Mario's "bite," but he had never thought Ellen would be the victim.

As he raced down the corridor after her, it occurred to him that he ought to be beating Mario into a pulp right about now, yet he put the excellent notion aside for the moment. He couldn't lose Ellen.

Though she was running down the hallway, he caught her easily and spun her around to face him. He expected to see tears, but there were none. Instead, her face was tight with lack of emotion. Somehow, that was more frightening.

"Ell, they were incredibly stupid in there," he said, grabbing her shoulders. "I'm sorry, so sorry, if I hurt you by not jumping to your defense right away. But I just couldn't believe any one of them would even listen to that crap—"

"You . . . I thought you believed Mario."

"What!" He pulled her to him. "Never. Granted, he took me by complete surprise with his accusation. He took everyone in there by surprise. I know I was gaping, but I couldn't believe he would actually try such a ridiculous line. And then when I looked around and saw the relatives believing him . . . I'm sorry my family hurt you like that. If any of them had an ounce of logic, they'd see all the holes in his story."

She sobbed once, then wrapped her arms around him. "You looked so . . . I don't know, like you were doubting."

"I was doubting Mario's sanity for telling such an idiotic lie. I love you, Ell. I would never doubt you."

"Thank you," she whispered.

He swallowed back his emotions. He wanted to carry her away from all the hurts in the world, but he knew it was impractical. Still they were a few steps away from the back entrance to his office and the small corner of privacy that office offered. He escorted her to the hall door, unlocked it, and waved her inside. He followed behind her. Once he'd swung the door closed and the automatic lock had clicked shut, he wasted no more time.

"I love you." He pulled her into his kiss, letting his actions speak for him.

At first, she was pliant in his arms. Then she was explosive, her mouth melding with his. He came back to his senses when he tasted a salty wetness. He lifted his head to find tears trickling down her cheeks.

She managed a smile. "You were right. He did take everyone by surprise. To tell you the truth, I don't even know if my father has stock in that company—"

"You don't need to explain."

She put a finger to his lips. "I just want you to know. My father . . . he has stock everywhere. I've barely spoken to him or my mother since my divorce. I love you, Joe, so much. But . . . your family. They'll never believe me."

"They will, if I have something to say about it. And I do." He grinned. "Though right now, they're probably in there voting to fire me. So now we're both on the outs with our families. And frankly, my dear, I don't give a damn. Let's go start a family of our own. The sofa right next to the door here will do nicely."

"Joe!"

"Or we could get kinky and try the coffee table."

Her mouth was open in an O of astonishment, and he took advantage of it. In the midst of the kiss, the sound of the door knob being slowly turned caught his attention. He lifted his head and put a finger against Ellen's thoroughly kissed lips. Her eyes widened as he pointed to the knob. They both looked and saw it turn twice more.

It didn't take a genius to guess who was testing the door, and what he was after. Mario, having created chaos in the board room, was now boldly taking advantage of it to steal the CEO's copy of the recipe right out of his own safe. A scratching sound reached their ears. Joe realized the lock was being picked. He had no time to consider the how and why of Mario's actions.

"Quiet as a mouse, and we'll catch him," he whispered to Ellen.

He pushed her behind his desk and they crouched down. "There's stationery on the shelves under the computer," he said. "Get a plain envelope, shove a piece of paper in it and write 'City Wage Tax Agreement' on the front."

" 'City Wage Tax Agreement?' " she whispered back.

"Just do it and quick."

The bookcases lining the wall behind them held more than books, and Joe tilted down a fake section, exposing the latest in digital safes. He keyed in the code numbers, and the tumblers clicked open. Among the contents was a plain white envelope with the words "City Wage Tax Agreement" on it. Joe exchanged the fake one Ellen had whipped together for the original and shut the safe closed, then he tilted up the artificial book section. He shoved the original envelope in Ellen's hands.

"Go out by the secretary's office and get my family."

"Is this—"

"It isn't Ragu's. I know you'll keep it safe. Now, dammit, Ell, go and get help!"

She scrambled away from him and was out of the other door. He allowed himself one quick grin at her astonishment and her speed as he dove into the private bathroom. He left the door cracked, praying it wouldn't be noticed.

It seemed forever before he heard his private outer door finally open. Now that he had time to think, he wondered why Mario was making such an attempt now and not before. He had no idea how Mario would open the safe, or if he even could, then he heard the familiar beeps of the code being keyed in. Rage clouded his vision at the thought that Mario had the code. But how? Someone had to have given it to him. That was the only way. But if he had the codes, then why hadn't he gone for the copy before this? He set the question aside temporarily as the safe clicked open. Joe could hear no more though. He counted to ten, hoping that was enough time to literally catch Mario red-handed.

He strode boldly into the room. Mario, squatting down in front of the safe, plain white envelope in hand, fell over backward at the sight of his older cousin.

"Hello," Joe said cheerfully. "And did we find what we wanted?"

"Ahh . . . I . . ." Mario stared at him, his mouth gaping.

The office door swung open and Joe Carlini, Senior stepped into the room, followed by the rest of the board members.

"What's all this about—"

Everyone froze and stared at Mario sitting on the floor in front of the open safe.

"Ohmigod! That's . . . that's . . ." Joe's father stuttered. "Ohmigod! The recipe! He's stealing the recipe!"

"No!" Mario's mother gasped. "There's proof of

his innocence in the safe. He told me. That's why I . . . Oh, no. No, no . . ."

She burst into tears, while Mario's father cried out in despair.

Throwing the envelope down, Mario jumped to his feet and bolted for the private office door, making a last desperate attempt to escape. Joe cursed and leaped after him, but his knee caught on the edge of the desk. He yelped in agony and grabbed his injured knee, helpless to stop his cousin. Mario laughed.

Before anyone else could move, Ellen plowed into Mario from the side. Mario staggered and pushed her to the floor, while trying to regain his balance. He failed and fell into the coffee table instead.

Sitting up, Ellen pushed the hair out of her eyes and surveyed the tangle of man and table.

"Next time you decide to accuse a Kitteridge of stealing, think again." She turned to Joe and grinned. "I believe we'll have to use the sofa."

He laughed.

She stood up and pulled a crumpled envelope out of her skirt pocket. "The real McCoy. It got a little squished. Sorry about that."

"She has the recipe?" Joe's mother asked, her voice incredulous.

"Of course," Joe said, gazing at Ellen. "I trust my lady. With everything."

She flew into his arms. "I love you, Joe."

He held her tightly. "You better."

"Thank you, Ellen," Joe's father said, drawing their attention. "I believe all of us owe you an apology."

"And more," Joe's mother said.

It was another painful half-hour before Mario and his parents left the room. Mario confessed that he had accepted a large sum of money, half up front, from PrimaVera, their biggest competitors, for the recipe. But he was unrepentant to the end.

The rest of the Board and family members went back to the board room, sitting around the only table that could accommodate them all. Joe, sitting next to Ellen and holding her hand, admitted prosecution was out of the question for Mario. This was a family matter, after all.

"As soon as you left to go after Ellen," Joe's father said, "Mario excused himself to use the bathroom. Once calmer heads prevailed, we realized that Mario hadn't brought his fears about Ellen to anyone before today. Neither did he mention being approached by the other company. Even Mary and Michael couldn't dispute that, although Mary tried. We're all very sorry for any pain this might have caused you, Ellen. You saved the recipe. How can we ever thank you?"

Joe smiled when she squeezed his hand and said, "I'll think of something."

There was, however, a serious matter of security.

"Mario had the codes to the office safe, Dad," he said, eyeing his father sternly. "I only gave that code to you."

His father's eyes widened, then narrowed. He rounded on his wife. "And I gave it to your mother, in case something ever happened to me."

Mrs. Carlini shrugged helplessly. "I was worried

that if something happened to all three of us, no one could get into the safe, so I gave the code to your brother, Thomas. That was all right, wasn't it?"

Joe groaned. So did his father.

"I thought it best to give it to Michael," Thomas began, looking guilty. "He must have given it to Mary. And of course, she told Mario—"

"Wait a minute!" Joe exclaimed, his suspicions aroused by a few more guilty faces looking away from Thomas. "Is there anyone in this room who does *not* know the code to the office safe?"

Lettice Kitteridge raised her hand. No one else joined her.

"Well, I don't," she said, lowering her hand.

Joe didn't bother to reply. He was staring at Ellen.

"I saw the first two numbers," she said in a small voice.

"Wonderful," he muttered. "Even I'm giving it away. I guarantee there's going to be a few changes in security around here."

"You can settle that later, Joseph," Lettice interrupted. "Right now, I want to know when the wedding date is."

"Grandmother!" Ellen exclaimed. "Who said anything about marriage?"

"I did," Lettice said promptly. "I worked my tail off to get you matched up with Joseph—after I approved of him, of course. So, Joseph, answer my question."

Joe looked at Ellen and smiled. "Anytime Ellen says."

She smiled back. "Anytime Joe says."

He raised her hand to his mouth and kissed it.

Lettice's eyes gleamed with anticipation. "Mrs. Carlini and I will take care of everything. You two just show up."

Ellen shook her head with mock despair. "I give up."

"About time, my love," Joe murmured to her. Louder he said, "I think we can manage that."

"After Atlantic City," Ellen reminded him.

"Right, after Atlantic City."

"What's in Atlantic City?" Thomas asked.

They burst into laughter.

Epilogue

Ellen watched the tall six-year-old boy plunge into the water, his swan dive more of a belly flop.

He surfaced instantly and yelled, "How was that, Mom?"

"Perfect, Jason," she lied, and grinned with pride at her older son. She wondered if Greg Louganis started out this way. With his dark hair and good looks, Jason reminded her so much of Joe.

"Mommy, watch!"

She turned in time to see a smaller boy race to the pool's edge and literally fall in. Her heart leaped in instant remembrance, then she relaxed back in her lounge chair. This four-year-old broke through the water and splashed around playfully, his water safety ring secure around his waist. This five-year-old now, Ellen corrected herself, smiling. Today was John's birthday, but he wasn't waiting for his guests to arrive on this hot August afternoon for his pool party. The pool might make her nervous, but she was determined not to hold her children back.

"You nearly splashed me, young man!" Lettice called from her adjacent lounge chair. She glared at her youngest great-grandson. He giggled, clearly unafraid. Lettice subsided into a grin and turned to her granddaughter. "I love them both dearly, but I expect a girl this time, you know."

"I know." Ellen touched her swelling abdomen and smiled. A girl would be nice. Her household was beginning to be overrun with males.

"I see he couldn't wait," Joe commented, as he came out onto the patio.

"Just like you," Ellen said, smiling.

"By the way, Ellen," Lettice said, "I hope you are not roller skating in your condition."

Dead silence greeted her in answer.

"Ellen!"

"It's good exercise," Ellen said defensively.

"The kid could grow up like me, and be a total klutz on skates," Joe reminded Lettice, who harrumphed her disapproval.

Ellen gazed at her husband, who hadn't changed at all since the first time they'd met. She sighed and said, "I love you, klutz."

He bent over and kissed her soundly on the lips. Heat flooded her veins, just as it always did.

"Too bad we can't find the nearest cabana," he whispered.

"Mmmm." She pulled his mouth down to his again.

"Ugghhh! Kissing again."

They broke apart, laughing at the children's squeals of disgust.

"A few more years and neither will be making faces at kissing," Lettice said with satisfaction. "I'll be matchmaking for both of them."

"Poor souls," Joe said, grinning.

Ellen smothered her laughter. Lettice had become a noted matchmaker, whether her victims liked it or not.

Within minutes the guests began to arrive. The spacious home she and Joe now had in Bucks County was filled with Carlinis and Kitteridges. Ellen mingled with her in-laws, totally at ease and accepted. She had discovered, shortly after her marriage, that Joe's mother had been worried that Joe was just a fling for an ex-princess and hadn't wanted him to be hurt. However, everyone had been too busy coping with the aftermath of Mario and Joe's changes in the company to truly worry about her. The infamous Ellen Kitteridge was hardly infamous compared to their own troubles. Mario's parents had divested themselves from the company, and although it was best in the end, it had been upsetting for all of them. Mario had even surfaced on the competitor's payroll for a while.

Until he been caught switching cheaper materials for better and pocketing the difference, Ellen thought, watching several people dig into the antipasti she'd made.

"*Rigne Di Prosciutto!*" Uncle Thomas exclaimed, admiring the little puff pastries filled with minced ham.

"I was thinking of it for the gourmet line," Ellen said, praying they all liked it.

"I love it," Carol declared. "Hors d'oeuvres would

be a great addition. Busy women who need an elegant meal quick will go bonkers for them."

"Hard to believe my granddaughter has become a businesswoman," Lettice said, picking up one of the ham puffs. After devouring the morsel, she added, "And a darn good one at that."

Ellen laughed, remembering how she had held a small dinner party for Joe's parents and had made all Italian dishes, in an effort to please them. They had raved, and Joe had immediately added the main course, Osso Bucco, to the frozen food line. After that, she'd begun to visit the Research and Development kitchens. "To think I accidentally fell into it."

"You didn't fall into it," Joe said, curving his arm around her and pulling her close to his side. "You married into it."

Ellen Kitteridge-Carlini gazed up at her husband and grinned.

"Thank goodness."

Lettice Kitteridge smiled.

THE EDITOR'S CORNER

What an extraordinary sextet of heroes we have for you next month! And the heroines are wonderful, too, but who's paying all that much attention when there are such fantastic men around?

Iris Johansen is back with a vibrantly emotional, truly thrilling romance, **MAGNIFICENT FOLLY,** LOVESWEPT #342. Iris's man of the month is Andrew Ramsey. (Remember him? Surprised to reencounter him as a hero? Well, he is a marvelous—no, magnificent—one!) When this handsome, unusually talented, and sensitive man appears in Lily Deslin's life, she almost goes into shock. The intuitive stranger attracts her wildly, while almost scaring her to death. Abruptly, Lily learns that Andrew has played a very special, very intimate role in her life and, having appeared as if by magic, is on the scene to protect her and her beloved daughter Cassie. Before the danger from the outside world begins, Lily is already in trouble because Andrew is unleashing in her powerful emotions and a deep secret she's kept buried for years. Iris's **GOLDEN CLASSIC, THE TRUSTWORTHY RED-HEAD,** is now on sale. If you read it—and we hope you will—we believe you'll have an especially wonderful time with **MAGNIFICENT FOLLY,** as Andrew, Lily, and Cassie take you back to Alex Ben Rashid's Sedikhan.

Ivan Rasmussen is one of the most gorgeous and dashing heroes ever . . . and you won't want to miss his love story in Janet Evanovich's **IVAN TAKES A WIFE,** LOVESWEPT #343. The fun begins when Stephanie Lowe substitutes for her cousin as cook on board Ivan's windjammer cruise in Maine coastal waters. Descended from a pirate, Ivan sweeps Stephanie off her feet while laughing at her Calamity Jane performance in his galley. He had never thought of settling down until he embraced Stephanie, and she had never been made to feel cherished until Ivan teased and flirted with her. But Stephanie has her hands full—a house that's falling apart, a shrivelling bank account, and some *very* strange goings-on that keep her and Ivan jumping once they're back on terra firma. There is a teenager in this story who is an absolutely priceless character as far as those of us on the LOVESWEPT staff are concerned. We hope you enjoy

(continued)

her and her remarkable role in this affair as much as we did. Full of humor and passion, **IVAN TAKES A WIFE** is a real winner!

Imagine meeting a red-bearded giant of a man who has muscles like boulders and a touch as gentle as rose petals. If you can dream him up, then you have a fair picture of Joker Vandergriff, Sandra Chastain's hero in **JOKER'S WILD**, LOVESWEPT #344. We can only thank Sandra for taking us in this story back to delightful Lizard Rock, with its magical hot springs and its wonderful people, where Joker is determined to heal the injuries of former Olympic skater Allison Josey. He mesmerizes her into accepting his massages, his tender touches, his sweet concern . . . his scorching kisses. Her wounds are emotional as well as physical, and they run deep. Joker has to fight her demons with all his considerable power. Then, in a dramatic twist, the tables turn and Joker has to learn to accept Allison's gift of love. As heartwarming as it is exciting, **JOKER'S WILD** leaves you feeling that all is more than right with the world.

Rugged, virile, smart, good-looking—that's Nick Jordan, hero of the intense and warm romance **TIGRESS**, LOVESWEPT #345, by Charlotte Hughes. What a dreamboat this sexy peach farmer is . . . and what a steamy delight is his romance with Natalie Courtland, a woman he finds stranded on his property during a freak snowstorm. The cabin fever they come to share has nothing to do with going stir-crazy as the storm keeps them confined to his home; it has everything to do with the wild attraction between them. Beyond their desire for each other, though, they seem to have nothing in common. Natalie is a divorce lawyer in Atlanta, and Nick has forsaken the world of glamorous condos, designer clothes, sophisticated entertainment, for a way of life he considers more real, more meaningful. How they resolve their differences so that love triumphs will keep you on the edge of your chair. A true delight first to last!

Ooh, la, la, here comes Mr. Tall, Dark, and Handsome himself—Dutton McHugh, Joan Elliott Pickart's devastating hero of **SWEET BLISS**, LOVESWEPT #346. When Bliss Barton wakes up with her first ever hangover, she finds a half-naked hunk in her bed! She could die of

(continued)

mortification—especially when she recognizes him as one of her brother's rowdy buddies. Dutton is not her type at all. Careful, cautious, an outsider in her family of free spirits, Bliss has kept her wild oats tightly packed away—while Dutton has scattered his to the four winds. When her family misunderstands the relationship between Bliss and Dutton, and applauds what they imagine is going on, Bliss decides to make it real. The hilarious and touching romance that follows is a true joy to read!

Fayrene Preston outdoes herself in creating her hero in **AMETHYST MIST,** LOVESWEPT #347. Brady McCullough is the epitome of rugged masculinity, sex appeal, and mystery. When Marissa Berryman literally falls into his life, he undergoes a sudden and dramatic change. He is wild to possess her ... not just for a night, but for all time. The confirmed bachelor, the ultimate loner has met his fate. And Marissa, who goes up in flames at his touch, is sure she's found her home at last. Parted by the legacies of their pasts, they have to make great personal journeys of understanding and change to fulfill their destiny to love. A breathlessly exciting love story with all of Fayrene's wonderfully evocative writing in full evidence!

I reminded you about Iris's **GOLDEN CLASSIC,** but don't forget the three other marvelous reissues now on sale ... **SOMETHING DIFFERENT,** by Kay Hooper; **THAT OLD FEELING,** by Fayrene Preston; and **TEMPORARY ANGEL,** by Billie Green. What fabulous romance reading. Enjoy!

With every good wish,

Carolyn Nichols

Carolyn Nichols
Editor
LOVESWEPT
Bantam Books
666 Fifth Avenue
New York, NY 10103